John Creasey – Master Storyteller

Born in Surrey, England in 1908 into a poor family in which there were nine children, John Creasey grew up to be a true master story teller and international sensation. Writing under multiple pseudonyms, his more than 600 crime, mystery and thriller titles have now sold 80 million copies in 25 languages. These include many popular series such as *Gideon of Scotland Yard, The Toff, Dr Palfrey and The Baron*.

Never one to sit still, Creasey had a strong social conscience, and stood for Parliament several times, along with founding the One Party Alliance which promoted the idea of government by a coalition of the best minds from across the political spectrum..

He also founded the Crime Writers' Association, which to this day celebrates outstanding crime writing. The Mystery Writers of America bestowed upon him the Edgar Award for best novel and then in 1969 the ultimate Grand Master Award. John Creasey's stories are as compelling today as ever.

BY THE SAME AUTHOR
Published or to be published by House of Stratus

GIDEON OF SCOTLAND YARD	(22 TITLES)
THE TOFF	(59 TITLES)
INSPECTOR WEST	(43 TITLES)
THE BARON	(47 TITLES)
DR. PALFREY	(34 TITLES)
DEPARTMENT 'Z'	(28 TITLES)

Gideon's Art

John Creasey

(writing as JJ Marric)

Copyright © 1971 John Creasey Literary Management Ltd

All rights reserved. No part of this publication may be reproduced, stored in a retrieval system, or transmitted, in any form, or by any means (electronic, mechanical, photocopying, recording, or otherwise), without the prior permission of the publisher. Any person who does any unauthorised act in relation to this publication may be liable to criminal prosecution and civil claims for damages.

The right of John Creasey to be identified as the author of this work has been asserted.

This edition published in 2010 by House of Stratus, an imprint of Stratus Books Ltd., Lisandra House, Fore Street, Looe, Cornwall, PL13 1AD, U.K.

www.houseofstratus.com

Typeset, printed and bound by House of Stratus.

A catalogue record for this book is available from the British Library and the Library of Congress.

ISBN 07551 - 2389 - 1
EAN 978 - 07551 - 2389 - 6

This book is sold subject to the condition that it shall not be lent, resold, hired out, or otherwise circulated without the publisher's express prior consent in any form of binding, or cover, other than the original as herein published and without a similar condition being imposed on any subsequent purchaser, or bona fide possessor.

This is a fictional work and all characters are drawn from the author's imagination. Any resemblance or similarities to persons either living or dead are entirely coincidental.

ACKNOWLEDGMENT

This book is dedicated to Lynn and Scoop, because they believe so much in art; and particularly because Lynn spent so much time helping me to clean the painting which is part of the plot.

Author's Note

While the general details of the galleries and museums in this book are accurate, I have in some cases taken liberties by introducing rooms which do not in fact exist, official positions which are imaginary, and, of course, many characters - all of whom are fictional and have no relation to any living persons, hard though I try to make them appear as flesh and blood.

I am most grateful to the officials at the various galleries mentioned in the book for their friendly help and guidance.

PAINTED INTO A CORNER

There was a second of stunned silence before Robin Kell's hand flashed to and from his jacket and the click of his knife sounded loud. He'd had enough. If the collector wouldn't agree to the exchange, then the girl, Christine, must die. Falconer tried to rush forward to protect his daughter, but the knife moved swift as light toward him, and into his belly. He felt a searing pain and staggered to one side, saw the knife flash again as Kell turned to use it on Christine.

Falconer's last memory before losing consciousness was of Gideon and his men storming the premises . . . .

1: The Method

"So it's worth a quarter of a million," Jenkins said.

"Pounds," remarked Slater.

"And I've a market," de Courvier stated, in his over precise voice. "We will get twenty-five thousand pounds *each*."

"I thought you said it was worth a quarter of a million," said Slater.

"It is. That's why it's worth twenty-five thousand pounds for each of us," retorted de Courvier. "In dollars, if you want to go for a nice long holiday out of this country."

"You mean you can sell it to the States?" asked Slater, scepticism sharp in his tone. "That's a new one on me."

"I did not say that I could sell it to the States," replied de Courvier. I said I had a market. We can collect twenty-five thousand pounds apiece, just for stealing it. My buyer will make a big profit, but does that matter?"

In a long pause, the three men looked at one another, Jenkins with a cigarette drooping from his protruding lower lip, Slater with a half-smoked cigar jutting from his thick and fleshy mouth, de Courvier prim, almost dandified, sitting well back in a winged Regency armchair with badly frayed arms. From outside came the noise of a pneumatic drill, unpleasantly close. Thin curtains, drawn, concealed the men and the tiny room from passers-by. Several women and some children went past, then a man, his steps slow and deliberate, and Slater looked up, suddenly and as if instinctively on the alert.

The man's steps faded, and Slater turned to face the others

again.

"Where would we have to deliver?" asked Jenkins.

"I would take it to the go-betweens and they will hold it. We will have it only for an hour or two," de Courvier said.

"Okay, but where will we keep it *in* that hour or two?" Jenkins frowned.

De Courvier shrugged his shoulders. "Anywhere we say."

"Here?"

"Why don't we decide how we're going to get it first?" Slater sounded impatient.

"And whether," put in Jenkins. "That's the question. Are we or aren't we? If you ask me, it's a tricky one."

"It's simple as kissing one's hand," de Courvier stated flatly.

"Don't you believe it, old pal." Jenkins moved from a small, armless chair rather like a car seat and crossed to a corner of the room in which there was a sink, a wooden draining board, some shelves and cups and saucers, instant coffee, and a half-empty packet of tea bags. He filled an electric kettle from the one tap and plugged it into a socket on the wainscoting, straightening up with a grunt. "Those museums are never easy."

"You don't have to blow a safe or pick a lock," de Courvier said. "You just go and take the picture."

"With how many looking on?" jeered Jenkins.

"We cause a distraction," de Courvier said. "The crowd goes to see what is going on in the next salon; even the attendants take a look. We'll have plenty of time to get the painting."

"It wouldn't work," Jenkins said.

"One of us could throw a fit" Slater suggested. "Or—"

"That old trick," Jenkins said. "Forget it. Do they have closed circuit television at the National Gallery?"

"No," said de Courvier. "Of that I am positive."

"If you don't like my way, why don't you suggest something better?" asked Slater nastily.

The kettle began to sing as Jenkins took some cups and put them on a tray. "There's a lot of lolly to spare. Three times twenty-five is seventy-five thousand, and if it's worth a quarter of a million there's a hundred and seventy-five thousand going to someone who's sitting pretty."

De Courvier leaned forward. "You know as well as I do that we couldn't sell it at its full value. We couldn't sell it at all if there wasn't an agent standing by who will take a great deal of risk. He knows he can get a hundred-thousand pounds. If he can get more, that's his good fortune."

After a long pause, Jenkins said, "Okay. I'll settle for twenty-five thou." The cigarette, now little more than a stub, still dangled from his lower lip. "But it's no use to me if I'm inside. Do you know what we'd get for this one?"

"Three years," Slater said.

"For taking an Old Master out of the National Gallery? That's worse than murder! It would be more like ten years, if you ask me."

"What's the difference?" demanded Slater. "We aren't going to be caught."

"We'll be caught if we do it your way," Jenkins said. The kettle was nearly boiling and he put teabags in a brown earthenware pot and, timing the moment of true boil perfectly, poured in the water. Then he put the kettle on the draining board. "You both take sugar?" he asked.

"Not for me," Slater said, slapping his rounded belly. "I'm putting it on again."

"Courvy?" asked Jenkins.

"Neither sugar nor milk, thank you," de Courvier answered.

Jenkins poured out the tea, moved the cups to one side to make room for a tin of biscuits, then brought the tray over to his companions. They each took a cup. De Courvier bit firmly into a chocolate biscuit, while Jenkins put a whole one into his mouth and took the cigarette out, almost in the same movement.

"So what are we going to do?" asked Slater, at last. He was a short, thickset man, his lack of height apparent even when he sat.

"I do not think we need to discuss it further," said de Courvier, still sitting prim and upright. "Obviously, I shall have to find someone else to do this work for me."

"What the hell do you say that for?" asked Slater.

"This is not a matter where we can have indecision or difference of opinion," replied de Courvier sulkily. "Jenkins does not want to have any part in this. He would no doubt come in if you and I decided to work together but he would have no confidence, and that would lead to disaster. The wise thing is to forget it."

"That's great," Slater growled. "That's right up my street, that is. Twenty-five thousand quid put under my nose and then snatched away before I can get it. That's the kind of deal I really like, I *don't* think."

After a pause, Jenkins said: "Show me a way to do it with a good chance of getting the picture and I'm with you. But no fits, and no crowd scenes." He drank the remainder of his tea in a gulp and put the cup back on the tray. "You know me. The coolest nerve in the business."

"It's why I came to you," de Courvier said. "But if you're half-hearted, it is no use."

"Just show me the method," Jenkins demanded.

Slater moved his head slowly, revealing how thick his neck was, how it bulged over the ill-fitting coat, his eyes - sharp grey eyes - darting from side to side.

"You got any ideas?" he asked de Courvier.

"There is a way," de Courvier replied slowly, "a very good way. We need three to work inside, each for a few seconds. Once the picture has been removed, it is only a matter of getting it out of the gallery. I will do that. And I will take it straight to the agent and collect the money."

"Who's the agent?" Slater asked.

"A man prepared to take risks," de Courvier answered.

"What's the method?" Jenkins asked.

"Are you really prepared to play your part?" de Courvier

asked him.

"If I like the method, I'll play," said Jenkins. And after a pause, while he stared at de Courvier, he added: "More tea?"

"No, thank you." De Courvier placed the tips of his fingers together and looked almost priestlike. "The picture is thirty-five inches high and thirty inches wide. It has recently been cleaned and will roll easily. If the canvas is cut first along the bottom and then on both sides, tight with the frame, it will stay in position, because it is still hanging from the top. Is that understood?" He got up and went to a briefcase near the door, opened it, and took out a small picture in a plain wooden frame. He moved across to a calendar hanging from a nail over the tiny mantelshelf, took the calendar down, and hung the picture. The others edged toward him. De Courvier was taller than Jenkins by two or three inches, Jenkins taller than Slater by half a foot. Jenkins's hair seemed as if it had been plastered onto his head, Slater's was thick, black, and bushy, but there was a bald patch about the size of a small pineapple slice, and the patch was startlingly white.

With the picture in position, de Courvier took a razor blade in a special holder from an inside pocket, and made one crosswise movement at the bottom of the picture and one downward slash at each side. The picture itself went slack and looked a little crumpled, but did not roll up.

"You see?" de Courvier asked.

"I see," Jenkins said, nodding.

"Oke," Slater said, also nodding.

"When these three cuts have been made, the picture will be free except at the top," de Courvier went on. "Then—" He raised his hand and, apparently doing no more than mopping his forehead, pulled the canvas with his free hand. It came away, curling. With a dexterous twist, he rolled and stuffed it under his coat, and as if by magic another roll appeared in his right hand. As this unrolled, he pressed the corners against the empty space, and turned away.

"Strewth!" exclaimed Jenkins.

"Good," said Slater. "Not bad at all, I will say that. But it would take minutes!"

"One slash at a time," retorted de Courvier.

"What?"

"One slash at a time, at agreed intervals. They won't notice that; there won't be anything *to* notice unless you go very close. And only the last cut needs the expert."

"You?" asked Slater.

"Yes," answered de Courvier. "I have done it before, and I keep in practice."

"Strewth!" exclaimed Jenkins again. "It could *work*."

"Listen to me," de Courvier said, and in these moments he seemed to tower in stature above the others. "The visitors to all museums and galleries are constantly on the move. The same people never stay in one room for long; ten or fifteen minutes is average, and there is a constant change of visitors. So one of us cuts the bottom - all he seems to do is run his hand along the frame; he doesn't actually touch it. The attendant might see him but at a distance no damage will show. The attendant would notice if the same man came back and did the same thing, but he wouldn't be likely to notice a different man, and all you two have to do is make the cuts. Then I come in, and I can make the switch in ten seconds. Or even less."

"No one will even know the picture's missing," breathed Slater.

De Courvier was looking at Jenkins, who asked with great deliberation: "Who makes the third cut?"

"You do the first *and* the third," answered de Courvier. "For the first visit, you wear a beard."

Very slowly, Jenkins nodded; and for the first time he parted his lips enough to show his teeth in a strangely brilliant smile.

"How about getting out of the place?" asked Slater.

"I have planned that exactly, too," said de Courvier. "There will be no problem at all."

He sat down again, erect as ever, and began to talk.

While the three men planned the theft of one of the most valuable and renowned pictures in London's National Gallery, George Gideon, the Commander of the Criminal Investigation Department at New Scotland Yard, was sitting in his office and looking through some files which had been brought to him from Records. Each file was a dossier on a different man; each had a foolscap-sized form which gave details of age, height, habits, of everything which might help him to be identified, including a full set of finger and thumb prints of each hand. There were five files in all, and each was of a man with a criminal record as long as his arm. Each man was out of prison, and each was capable of having committed a crime which had taken place only the night before in an obscure art gallery in Chelsea. The value of the paintings that had been stolen was less than a thousand pounds and the five seldom worked for chicken feed; but if they were out of prison, out of work, and out of luck, any one of them might have thought the Chelsea job worth doing.

Gideon studied each with a closeness which characterized him. He knew four of the five in person, for each had been tried and convicted during his period as Commander, and in his position practically every criminal tried at the London Assizes was known to Gideon.

One of the men was a Leslie Jenkins.

Gideon read of his dozen convictions, from petty larceny when he had been seventeen to armed robbery when he had been thirty, seven—no, eight years ago. He had been one of a gang which had stolen art treasures from a country house and been caught trying to sell them in London. There was a note which read:

Earned full remission. Released 18th January 1970
Address: 14, Sonata Street, Lambeth, S.E.1

"Sonata" was an unusual name for a street, and it sent Gideon's thoughts in a completely different direction: to his daughter

Penelope. She was making slow headway as a concert pianist and was practicing a Beethoven sonata at home with a single-mindedness which nearly drove the rest of the family mad, although there was a conspiracy among them to show bright and smiling faces and to assure her that they enjoyed every moment. She was to play the piece at the Albert Hall in a week's time. Only a week more of forbearance, Gideon thought with a wry smile. Her success or failure with it would have an important effect on her future engagements, could lead her to remarkable success for a girl of. . .

Girl of. . .

He must not forget, she was twenty-five! He knew it well. Strange that he could forget; could even forget that his chief aide, Alec Hobbs, seemed deeply in love with her. One tended to shut certain facts out of one's mind instinctively.

Once again, then, he had been thinking of Penny as a girl. *Twenty-five!* His other daughters had married at that age; he had a grandchild - two grandchildren - on the way. And he still thought of them all as girls.

He sat back, more than a little rueful, then, making a conscious effort, forced his mind back to Leslie Jenkins. He recalled that Jenkins had a daughter of about the same age as Penelope; actually a young girl at the time of her father's arrest and trial! Her mother had died - or had she deserted Jenkins? She certainly hadn't been in evidence at the time of the sentence. Gideon could remember talking to the officers in charge of the case about the girl. There had been some suggestion of sending her to a home, but in the end she had been taken in by an aunt. What was her name, now? He made an effort to recollect it but could not do so.

The ring of a telephone bell made him start, and took his mind off the girl. The call was a trifle: would he be available in three weeks' time to give away some prizes at the Sports Club, on the evening of the Metropolitan Police Force Table Tennis Championships?

"Glad to," Gideon said. He jotted a note on a pad for transfer later to his diary, then sat back and said aloud: "Lucy, *that* was her name. Lucy Jenkins."

2: Lucy

Lucy Jenkins brushed her fair hair back from her forehead and stood away from the picture she was about to clean. It was astonishing how much dirt had accumulated in a few years and stuck to the varnish. This picture, according to the slip on the back, had been restored only twelve years before. Where on earth had it been to become so dirty?

She frowned, wrinkling her forehead, as she took the picture out of the old gilt frame. It was a modern painting and not a very good one, but she had a feeling that there was another painting beneath it.

Very soon she knew that she was right. Nervously but skilfully she cleaned off first the dirt at one corner, then the top layers of paint; she went on doing this until at last she could see most of the original picture - a country scene with three figures in the foreground - but as soon as the water she was washing it with dried, the picture faded.

She had bought the painting with a load of frames and prints from a man who had just cleared out an attic. Most of the pictures and prints were now tidied away, and entered in the Purchase Book. She had paid only five pounds for the lot.

Some of the paint of this particular picture had been rubbed away, showing not canvas but cracked varnish beneath, so she had been intrigued by it. Now she had proved that a hidden picture existed, and she knew it was in very fine perspective. She dusted it over carefully, planning to check whether it had ever been relined. The varnish over the old painting was very cracked. You could often judge a picture from the condition of the *craquelure*. She stood back, then picked up a big bottle of turpentine substitute, dipped in a swab of cotton wool, and slowly covered the whole picture. The colours and the design, of two women and a man, came up beautifully, but soon faded. She studied the corners, then cleaned a tiny patch of sky and the branch of a tree with two birds on it - that portion was one to test for relining.

She dipped a sponge in soapy water, and cleaned the corner again; then she took up a smaller bottle, labelled "dictate," dipped in a little swab at the end of a pencil-sized stick, and spread the mixture carefully over the corner, left it for a moment, then dabbed it off with the turps substitute and put on the mixture again. She mustn't leave it on too long; in restoring it was on, off, on, off, on, off, until at last the varnish was really off and the original paint was revealed.

That blue!

Those birds - hawks, they looked like.

The green of the leaves - it looked almost as if she could pick them!

Lucy Jenkins was very thin; her flaxen hair and blue eyes made her look Scandinavian, but in fact she was an Angle from a long way back, which accounted for her fair skin and the pink tinge to her cheeks. Unlike her father, she had well-shaped lips, and her chin was square, not thin and narrow like his. She had short but very thick eyelashes; had they been dark, they would have looked false.

Aloud, she said, "It's lovely."

She was alone, not only in the room at the back of the shop in King's Road, Chelsea, but in the shop as well. She worked for an elderly man named Jacob Fisk and his semi-invalid wife, minding the shop, cleaning pictures and frames, putting on new cords or wires. She had been doing this for several years now; it paid her all she needed and she was as nearly happy as she had ever been.

She had a single room at the back of the first floor of the

premises, and cooked and cleaned for herself, as well as helping out when Mrs. Fisk wasn't well.

When she had first come here, she had not known much about the work, although she had some familiarity with it, for her father had once been a runner for small picture dealers and galleries in London. She had known even as a child that under the double bed in her parents' room stolen pictures had been stored, and she had often seen her father doing what she was doing now - cleaning the corner of a picture to find out what really was under the varnish. She could half remember the smell of oil paints, thinners, wood, and canvas which there had been in a tiny shed in the back yard of her parents' home.

In a way, that was why she had taken this job: because of the sharp, penetrating odours.

She was careful, indeed painstaking, and she had an instinctive liking for old pictures, old prints - in fact, for anything old. When she had first come, she had had no idea of values, but she could now distinguish between a Chelsea and a Worcester figurine, could tell a genuine Hepplewhite or Chippendale from an imitation, could judge the value of repaired pieces, and particularly could distinguish a genuinely old painting from a new one, and a good one from a bad.

Only once had Old Fisky found a truly valuable picture, and after buying it for five pounds he had sold it for nearly four thousand. She could recall the excitement on his face when he had realized what he had bought, how newspaper reporters and photographers had flocked to the tiny shop, and ever since that day she had been on the lookout for something similar. It was not that she expected it, simply that she accepted the possibility and never forgot to check. Several times she had put a picture aside, hopefully, for Fisk, but each time she had discovered only a copy or a painting in the same school as one of the Old Masters.

"It's very funny," she repeated to the empty room. "Why would anyone paint this over old varnish without giving it a proper cleaning? Talk about *craquelure,* I'll bet my life that paint is real *old*. Those colours!"

She felt a tremor of excitement as she cleaned off a little more. Mixture on, pause, off with turps, pause, on - off - on - off. There was blue and grey in the corner, and then a touch of brown and green; it was an outdoor scene, trees and sky and clouds, and the people certainly didn't have much on in the way of clothes. She drew back and studied it again, almost touching the wall behind her. The room was little more than a passage, but it had one big north window and the light was perfect. On the bench which ran from wall to wall were other pictures, bottles of turpentine, rags, old canvases, frames, wood for framing and repairs; she was oblivious of everything but the picture now propped up against the wall.

She turned it over and read the tag; there was no doubt about the date of cleaning of the picture which had been on top: twelve years ago. The back of the canvas wasn't really dirty. Her heart gave a sudden lurch as she admitted the obvious possibility to herself: that the canvas had been painted over and relined so as to make the one underneath a kind of sandwich. Of course some artists painted over old pictures because they couldn't afford a new canvas, but usually it was to hide the one underneath.

She was confused, but very alert and very curious as she put the picture face downward on the bench.

She picked up a glazier's knife and prised the canvas loose; and when she first touched it with her fingers she felt another twinge of excitement, for it was very thick - thick and stiff as a board. She carried the picture closer to the window, and studied it.

Now she was sure. There were two linings, a new one to conceal the old one. No one covered both back and front because they couldn't afford canvas!

Everything she had learned about such a situation as this crowded into her mind. There were several ways of sticking canvases together, but the great danger was that if the picture was of any value, it could be damaged. One needed special solvents to separate the layers of varnish without causing damage, and she was not in any way an expert. It was exasperating, because Old Fisky would not be back for at least twenty-four hours, perhaps not until after the weekend. Not often impatient, she was edgy and disappointed; *was* there a picture of great value, even of modest value there? Had she made a real discovery?

She sighed and took the picture to a rack against a wall and placed it with half a dozen others, all of which needed attention from Old Fisky. Then she picked up a small Scottish Highland scene, quite dirty but not unusual. Cleaning it, she estimated the price the old man would ask for it. This wasn't one of her buys. The old man had bought the whole of the contents of a cottage for a song, sold off the large furniture and the modern pieces to second hand dealers, and had already made a profit. This little picture would fetch fifteen or twenty pounds. She wondered what he did with his money; he must be worth a small fortune.

And if she *had* made a discovery, he would see that she got her share. He wasn't mean, she could say that for him. She had quite a nice little balance in the Post Office Savings Bank, already put aside for a rainy day.

She had been in the back of the building for at least an hour when the shop doorbell rang, and she went out to see who it was. It was a man she recognized - Red Thomas, a middle-aged man with a red shirt and grizzled hair, a runner for the West End galleries who was always looking for snips.

"Hallo, Lucy," he said. "Anything for me today?"

"There's a copy of a Vermeer," she began quickly; customers often made her feel nervous.

"I don't want any copies," he interrupted. "Is the old man in?"

"No, he won't be back until later." Lucy never told anyone how long she could be alone and in charge, or that the place would be empty, but for her, at night.

The runner was going through some pictures stacked against

the wall, obviously looking for something specific, but he didn't say what. His clothes were threadbare and yet well-brushed and pressed. Lucy straightened some oddments of porcelain and china on the shelves. Though the shop was small and in need of painting, she kept it meticulously tidy.

At last, the runner stopped his searching and asked, "Anything in the back?"

"You know Mr. Fisk never keeps anything in the back if it's priced and ready for sale," she answered.

"There might be just the thing I'm looking for," he persisted. "Let me have a look through the back room and I'll see there's a fiver in it for you."

"Mr. Thomas," Lucy replied firmly, "everything we've got is in the shop. Please don't make difficulties."

"Oh, all right." The man stood very still, facing her. His expression hardened. "You're as stubborn as your old man," he said, with an edge of cruelty in his voice. "I hope it doesn't land you in the same place."

He spun on his heel and strode out, while Lucy stood white-faced, staring at the window but not really seeing him. She hated being reminded that her father was an ex-convict. She tried desperately to forget it but somehow never could. Often it was the shop which reminded her, the fact that her father had at one time done a lot of business with Old Fisky.

On the other side of the road, two policemen passed, one of them speaking into his little walkie-talkie radio. The other one looked across at her. She hadn't any doubt, he was looking at *her:* was it with suspicion?

She went back to the workroom. It was no use telling herself that she was being ridiculous, that there was nothing to suspect her for. She was always conscious of policemen and uneasy in their presence. And she was so upset by Red Thomas's remark she did not give the mystery picture a thought until, half an hour later, she locked both back and front doors and went upstairs.

Then she thought, It might have been stolen. And the

possibility troubled her very much indeed.

The two policemen who had been in King's Road, Chelsea, walked together into the Chelsea Divisional Station, the Headquarters of the CD Division, about quarter to eight that night, and filed their reports. There was nothing much in any of them, but the younger of the two, Police Constable Wilfred Chivers, made a routine comment.

> "Red Thomas was in Jake Fisk's shop in N.K.R. this afternoon - 4.40 until 5.00 P.M. approx."

After leaving Lucy, Red Thomas walked for ten minutes, looked into another shop, and then caught a bus back to the West End. He sat on top, smoking, watching the streets and the crowds perfunctorily, thinking of the shops and the pictures he had seen, wondering what he could offer to West End buyers who might give him an advance on commission. He had been in the art business most of his life. He knew a great deal about paintings, especially of the main English and Dutch schools, but he was only on the fringe of the trade. He had no heart for paintings, no feel or love for them. To him they were simply coloured canvasses or panels, and he saw no intrinsic beauty in them.

He earned a reasonable living but seldom made big money, because he had a curious characteristic: while he had a very good eye for the artist or school a particular dealer was interested in, he had no eye at all for a find.

He was, within his own limits, honest, and he had never been in prison, though he knew of a great number of men, like Leslie Jenkins, who had been inside severed times but, when out in the everyday world, had made fortunes, only to waste them on gambling or drinking. And he envied these men as he envied anyone who made more money than he.

He got off the bus, turned in to a narrow lane off Bond Street, and went into the Oriole Gallery, where a silver-haired woman sat at a small desk. The Oriole Gallery specialized in paintings of birds and animals; its walls were crowded with oil paintings, watercolours, and prints.

"Hallo, Mrs. Bessell," Red said. "I'm back."

"So I see," Mrs. Bessell said dryly. "Did you find anything?"

"There's a fine pair of pheasants at Old Fisky's, King's Road," he said. "Real beauties, they are. I could get them for thirty if you like; you'd get fifty for them at least - a hundred, knowing you."

"I'd want to see them," Mrs. Bessell said. She wore pebble-lensed glasses, which diminished her attractiveness.

"Well, I don't know about that. They might not let me have them on approval, and if they know who wants them the price will go up. You know what these Chelsea dealers are like, Mrs. Bessell."

"I know they would want a deposit," the woman admitted. "I'll think about it, Red."

"I could get out there tonight," the man persisted. "Fisk lives over the shop, so there wouldn't be any difficulty. And I could have them here first thing in the morning." When the woman made no answer, he went on doggedly: "I might get them for twenty-five. I happen to know Fisk's a bit short of ready cash. He bought a big load a couple of weeks ago and—"

"I'll decide in the morning," Mrs. Bessell said; then, seeing the defeated expression on his face, her tone softened and she asked, "Short of a pound, Red?"

"You never said a truer word," he replied miserably.

Mrs. Bessell opened a drawer in her desk and took out a black metal cashbox.

"I'll give you an advance on the next job you do for me," she told him. "But I want preferential treatment. Do you understand?"

"Mrs. Bessell, you always get it. I swear you always get it."

Eagerly he took the two rather soiled pound notes she held out to him, looked nervously about the shop, then backed out. He disappeared, walking very fast toward Piccadilly. Traffic built up outside, and an impatient driver put a finger on his horn and kept it there.

When Red had gone, a door leading from a passage at the side of the gallery opened and a man stepped toward Flora Bessell, skin dark against hers as he bent to kiss her cheek.

"You've got the biggest heart in the business," he said.

Flora Bessell flushed with pleasure and tilted her head to look into the smiling eyes of her lover.

"Keep telling me that, Oily," she said, almost pleading.

Frederick Oliphant smiled again and squeezed her arm.

3: Gideon

George Gideon left his office at Scotland Yard late that evening, a little after seven o'clock. He walked, massive and almost forbidding, along the passage toward the main doors and the long flight of steps leading into the forecourt. There was something about the depth and breadth of his shoulders, his rather short neck, his broad, rugged, not unhandsome face, which could strike a kind of fear into those who saw him and served under him. He was aware of this, and disliked and almost resented it with one part of his mind, yet accepted and took advantage of it with another part. It was very good for discipline and it kept men on their toes. Often, he knew, he looked more forbidding when in fact there was no great worry or problem on his mind. This evening there was nothing to cause him particular concern; none of the investigations going through the Yard needed undue concentration.

His car was at the foot of the steps, and a detective officer stood by the door.

"Good night, sir."

"Good night."

"Lovely evening."

"Just right."

"Shouldn't go round Parliament Square if I were you," the man volunteered. He was middle-aged, old for a detective officer, only a few years younger than Gideon.

"Why not?" asked Gideon, settling in at the wheel.

"Doing something to the road," the other answered. "Cars

are jammed like sardines."

Gideon grunted, not very graciously, and drove onto the Embankment, turning left, not right toward Parliament Square and the Houses of Parliament. Big Ben, behind and out of sight, struck the quarter. Traffic on the far side was already slowing down, and above the shiny tops of cars and between the big red buses he could see the higher level of the London County Hall and, further along, some of the slender arches of Waterloo Bridge and the top of the new Shell buildings across the river. Trees hid the Festival Hall, and he could not see a single patch of water. In a strange way his mood had changed, entirely because of Parker, the detective officer he had just spoken to, who would never become a sergeant unless on sentimental or compassionate grounds. Any man at the Yard who knew a major road was up but could only describe it as "something" was an indifferent policeman. Gideon, unaware that his own thirst for knowledge was as natural as breathing, wanted to know what was being done.

He turned in to Northumberland Avenue and reached the traffic lights at Trafalgar Square. There traffic was much thinner; the homeward rush was over and the reverse-direction theatre rush had not yet started. There was something both soothing and satisfying about the scene, and he was glad of the wait at the red signal. Nelson's Column, recently cleaned, looked a little unreal as it rose from its guard of bronze lions. The square itself, its fountains playing, the pigeons strutting like an ill-disciplined army, was bathed in the evening light, tinged now with a warm pinky gold. The fountains were like waterfalls. Beyond, looking almost naked from *its* recent cleaning, was the National Gallery.

Soon, driving along King's Road and New King's Road, he passed the rows of second hand and antique shops, without noticing the one with the name "Jacob Fisk" on the fascia. He had no idea that Lucy Jenkins lived and worked there, but he realized one thing which he must have noticed before but which had not registered as it did now: practically every shop in this stretch of New King's Road sold antiques or garden furniture, masonry or pictures. This side of London was fast becoming an art and artists' colony on a much greater scale than the Chelsea of his youth; the trade that went on in this square mile must be enormous.

And because he was a policeman, he wondered whether the Yard had its finger as firmly on this area's pulse as it should. Where there was trade, there was crime; where there were small art dealers, there was a great risk of buying and selling of stolen goods. Although he lived nearby, he had not given much thought to the mushrooming of a business with such an obvious crime potential.

This area was covered by CD Division, and Jack White, the Superintendent in charge, was a good, solid, sound detective, but hardly a man with a flair. He would have to find a reason to talk to White. One could hardly expect the divisions to specialize, however, and the specialist in art at the Yard was Frobisher, Wally Frobisher, a much younger man, who had won swift promotion because of his knowledge of the art world. Frobisher was at the moment up in Manchester, helping the local police with the investigation of a theft of three small Watteaus from the Manchester City Museum.

There was another man, Thwaites, who had a less expert but much wider general knowledge, at the Yard. He might know much more about the present situation than Frobisher.

By the time Gideon reached his own street, Harrington Street, Fulham, close to the Hurlingham sports grounds, he had put Jack White and Frobisher to the back of his mind. He had a garage round the corner at the far end of the street. Neighbours were working in their gardens and many doors and windows were open; out here it seemed even more muggy than it had been in town. The front-room window of his own house was wide open, and he heard two or three bars of Beethoven's *Sonata in C Minor*. He broke into a smile, which broadened as he caught sight of Penelope sitting slantwise by the sitting-room window. Then he noticed that two or three neighbours were at their front gates, others at their windows, and none of them was talking.

They were, he thought, listening to Penelope.

Now that he was no longer in the car, he could hear much more clearly. Into the quiet there came a sudden clatter of a lawnmower, and one of two women at a gate said, "Oh, drat that man!"

The clattering went on, and now only those neighbours close to Gideon's house could hear Penelope playing. She was near the end, he knew, and he wondered how many more times she would go over the piece again this evening. A man at the window of the house next door, called, "Beautiful, Mr. Gideon, absolutely beautiful."

"Thank you," Gideon said. "You don't find it a nuisance, then?"

"A nuisance - that girl's playing? Good Lord, no!"

Gideon, highly pleased, turned into his gate and, glancing up, saw Kate, his wife, at the window of their bedroom. She raised a hand, then turned away; and when he stepped into the house, she was halfway down the stairs. She was a handsome woman with a fine figure; her hair was greyer than Gideon's, but with the blue rinse she had now, she looked much younger than he did.

Her face was smooth and unlined, and it was hard to believe that only a few months ago she had had serious heart trouble. For an agonizing moment, he relived the panic he had felt then - Kate, his wife, ill. She was fully recovered now, thank God.

She stood on the bottom stair, so that she seemed an inch or two taller than Gideon; and in fact, at five feet eight, she was tall for a woman.

Silence fell inside the sitting room as they met, and Kate, who had started to speak, uttered two or three words which sounded very loud, because the earlier words had been muffled by the piano music.

"It's a good thing that *someone feels he*—-"

When she stopped, her mouth was open, and Gideon

grinned, leaned forward to touch her cheek with his lips, then drew back and asked: "What's a good thing?"

"It doesn't matter," Kate said, in rare confusion. She looked at the sitting-room door, obviously expecting Penelope to come out, but when the door remained closed she took Gideon's arm and led him along the wide passage that ran by the side of the staircase, and into the living room. In these deep, narrow houses there was the front sitting room, then a smaller, connecting room used by many families as a dining room, and, beyond the passage, a big living room with kitchen and scullery opening off. Everything in this particular house was solid and of good quality, as well as being spick-and-span. "Oh, dear," Kate went on, half laughing, "I nearly put my foot in it, George."

"How?" inquired Gideon, deeply interested.

"Mr. Curtis has been complaining bitterly about Penny's practice, and Millicent's tried to calm him down, while I've been reassuring Penny. If she heard me say it's a good job someone feels he can enjoy piano music, Penny would have realized there's been trouble."

Gideon smiled. "It's a bit obscure, but I think I get you. One neighbour thinks she's wonderful and the other says she's driving him out of his mind."

"That's about it," said Kate.

"*Very* interesting," Gideon remarked, taking off his jacket. "Gosh, it's sticky tonight." He rolled up his shirt sleeves and went into the scullery, where he washed his hands under the tap. As Kate paused in the doorway, Gideon went on: "Have Curtis and Henshaw ever settled their argument over the service alley?"

Kate stared.

"Goodness!" she exclaimed. "I never thought of that!"

"Curtis complains, Henshaw hears about his complaints and is all sweetness and light, which is a way of getting at Curtis." Gideon reasoned. "And Penny gets squeezed in the middle, poor kid. Is she upset?"

"I don't think she knows anything has been said," Kate answered. "George—"

Gideon was back in the living room, taking whisky and glasses from a cupboard by the side of the fireplace. He was not a heavy drinker, but he had come increasingly to relax in the evening with a whisky-and-water. Kate came in with a small jug of water.

"For you?" asked Gideon

"No, I won't," said Kate. "George, I don't see how we can avoid complaints, and if Curtis makes an official one, or even comes banging on the door, it will upset Penny so much"

"Just a week to go," Gideon remarked. He sipped and dropped back into a large easy chair which looked as if it had been made for him. "We—"

"George," said Kate again, "you can't be glib about this."

Gideon, startled, echoed: *"Glib?"*

"You can't just push thought of it aside with a few casual words."

Gideon drank again, more deeply, hitched himself further up in his chair, and said with greater deliberation: "You were obscure before, dear. Now you're really confusing me! What am I supposed to be glib about?"

"Oh, I didn't really mean glib. I meant—"

"I was pushing something aside," said Gideon mildly.

"What, precisely?"

Kate, a little flushed, was spreading a white cloth over the big deal-topped table. She moved with natural grace, and Gideon never tired of watching her. She was a little thinner than she had been, her loss of weight especially noticeable at her waist, particularly when she wore a blouse and skirt, as she did now.

"There'll be more and more," she said, at last.

"More and more—oh—practice."

"Yes," Kate said with obvious relief. "When she's finished this sonata, she'll play another, and another, and another. That's inevitable, isn't it?"

"And the more successful she is, the more she'll have to

practicse."

"Yes, obviously."

"And the more our neighbour Curtis won't like it."

"It isn't only Curtis" replied Kate ruefully. "Several of the neighbours *have* asked rather pointedly when the concert is going to be held."

Gideon sipped, frowned, and half smiled.

"I know what you mean," he said. "'Doesn't Penelope play beautifully, Mrs. Gideon; when is she going to finish?' "

"I can't *really* blame them." Kate was putting knives and forks round the table, setting four places in all. "George—"

"We can't soundproof the sitting room," Gideon objected.

"We *could* soundproof the attic, or we could very nearly," answered Kate, and then she went on much too quickly, swallowing some of her words. "We only keep rubbish and our suitcases up there; half of it's boarded over, and I don't think the sound would travel far from the one small window. I shouldn't think it would cost—"

"Say, two hundred pounds," interjected Gideon.

"Oh, it couldn't be as much as that!"

"Yes, it could," answered Gideon. "Probably quite a bit more, too. Even if it were practicable."

"Oh, it is! I've had a good look round. And you know Alan Pryce-Davies, don't you - the cartoonist, I mean - *he's* soundproofed his room; he says it's the only way he could get any peace. I *can't* believe it would cost as much as two hundred pounds."

"Oh, well" said Gideon. "I suppose we can find out."

Kate's face lit up, making her look quite beautiful.

"May I, George?"

"Will you, love?"

"I'll make it my first job tomorrow," Kate promised. "George, she *is* our last daughter, and—"

"You don't have to sell me the idea," Gideon said gruffly. "Are we going to eat tonight?"

Kate, her eyes very bright, went past him to the kitchen,

pressing his shoulder firmly. Gideon finished his drink, then leaned back in his chair and dozed for the next few minutes, until Kate called out, "Well, if you're hungry." He opened his eyes to see the table laden with a steak pie with beautifully browned crust, three dishes piled up with boiled potatoes, carrots, and cabbage.

He smothered a yawn and got up as Kate, at the open door, called: "Penny!" As he reached the table, Penelope came in, tall but not so tall as her mother, dark hair drawn off her face, making her look a little too thin. Her eyes, also grey, lacked the brightness of Kate's.

"Hallo, Daddy. . . . Has it been a beastly day? . . . Oooh, what a lovely pie! . . ." He really *would* have to find her a practice room where she could play without being worried about the neighbours, he told himself, and reflected comfortingly that there wasn't much he needed to spend his income on these days.

Malcolm, the youngest of the family, came rushing in halfway through the meal, full of apologies about being late and having to go out again in twenty minutes.

"If you're going swimming—" began Kate.

"No, it's not swimming; it's work in the gym. Get the old muscles pepped up!" Malcolm stretched out his arms and flexed his biceps, brought his plate from the hotplate to the table to allow his mother to serve the main course, then helped himself to vegetables. Sitting opposite Penelope, he gave her a salute. "And how's the gorgeous pianoforte virtuoso today?"

Everyone laughed.

For the Gideons it was a pleasant, happy evening.

4: The Falconers

For the Falconers, who lived in Mayfair, it was a very different kind of evening. Christine Falconer, the only child, wondered whether she alone among the four present realized what kind of life they led, how unbelievably artificial it was. At certain times, she had a feeling that her mother was living under a great strain and somehow putting on an act; at others, she felt almost despairingly that her mother had become a kind of automaton, switched on as it were to defer exclusively to her husband's wishes.

Christine thought, looking down the long, highly polished Sheraton table at her mother, How *can* anyone so beautiful be so empty of emotions?

And she thought, looking toward the other end of the table at her father - in his high-backed chair, the arms of which always seemed a little too high so that he was continually knocking his elbows - How *can* anyone be so rich and so stupid?

Opposite her, his face softened by the candlelight from two big silver candelabra, sat Frederick Charles Stuart Oliphant, whom everyone knew as Oily. He had been virtually one of the family since she was quite tiny; she could not remember the great house without him. She had accepted him without thinking for so long that when at last her mind had opened to doubts and uncertainties about him and she had started to revalue her attitudes, it had been difficult to see him differently. He was now in his middle fifties, a little older than her father, and, of course, to her he had always seemed old. He was balding, with a round, pale face and a small rosebud of a mouth. She could never remember him being out of temper or ruffled or excited. He was the secretary, confidant, and friend of her father, and she knew that he was regarded as one of the great art experts of the world.

Davies, the butler, came in silently and offered more of the delicious apricot-and-peach flan, more of the rich Jersey cream: but no one wanted a second helping.

"We will have coffee in the drawing room," her father said.

"Very good, sir."

It was like a record player.

"Come along, dear," her mother called, as she had from the days when Christine had first been allowed to join them at the dinner table.

Oily moved and pulled her mother's chair back. Davies placed the port in front of his master. The candlelight made a cage of the dining table and the silver and the dishes, holding the gaze at eye level; now, above the glow, the pictures showed, each discreetly lit, each a portrait, each an Old Master, and each priceless. Christine stood up, feeling an almost overwhelming temptation to pick up a knife and hurl it at the nearest solemn face; instead, she turned away from the table and followed her mother out the door, at which Davies was standing, tall and stately and, like all of them, not quite real. She thought the whole nightly performance was like a charade in which the first prize went to whichever performer could show least expression.

They went out of the dining room into the hall.

Here were the landscapes: Gainsborough, Constable, Turner - paintings of rich beauty and great value. And here were the sculptures and the busts; it seemed to her as her mother walked past them that the marble and the granite, the bronze and the alabaster, were so much more real than the people who lived in her home.

"Mother," she said as they reached the open door of the drawing room.

"Yes, dear?"

"Mother, I've a headache. Do you mind if I go up to my room?"

"Your father will be very disappointed, Christine."

"Tell him I'm sorry, won't you?"

They stood facing each other for a few moments, and this was one of the rare occasions when Christine felt that the woman, not the automaton, was in front of her. Even then she was aware of the Dresden china perfection of her mother's skin, the brilliance of her eyes, all the subtlety of makeup, the elegant simplicity of the Balenciaga dress, the small diamond pin on her shoulder. The woman receded, the automaton, the work of art, taking her place, and a new thought crossed Christine's mind: that her mother had been made for her father, or else he had searched for her as he searched for every other rare piece in his collection.

"Christine, dear," her mother said. "You're not going out, are you?"

"I might—I might go out for a breath of fresh air."

"You haven't made any plans to see anybody?"

"No," Christine said. "But is there any reason why I shouldn't?"

"Well, you know, my dear, your father doesn't like some of the young people with whom you have been associating recently," her mother said. "I am sure you would be very wise not to see *them* or anyone else surreptitiously. You know how your father likes to have everything out in the open, don't you, dear?"

"Do you mean he's been—" Christine began, in sudden white heat of temper, but somehow she bit back the words "spying on me" and turned and hurried away. She felt in a turmoil, at the point of revolt against a life which was becoming increasingly intolerable.

She ran up the curving staircase, past recesses and alcoves in which stood vases and goblets, some of them chased gold and silver, some of the others jewel encrusted: The Italian (mostly

Cellini), the French, and the Spanish; a little farther up, where the stairs rounded, the Chinese of old dynasties were represented with vases and jade figures dug from ancient tombs. And on the landing were rare *objets d'art* from South America, from Russia, from Mexico. Every single piece was unique, every single piece of rare value.

She went hurrying by, oblivious of everything.

She turned in to her own suite, with a dressing room on one side and a bathroom on the other, all Regency, all beautiful, and hers. When she shut the door, she could at least shut the rest of the house off, the artificiality, the lifelessness.

My God! she thought. He's been having me watched. He's actually been spying on me!

She stood in the middle of the bedroom, feeling almost numbed. After what seemed a long time, she muttered, "I've got to get away! I simply must!"

Downstairs, her father and Oliphant went into the drawing room, where her mother sat looking at a television set. Coffee was on a low table in front of a long couch. Newspapers and magazines in great variety were in racks by each seat and chair.

"Oh, hallo, my dear" said Falconer. "Where's Christine?"

"She has a headache, Richard, and has gone to her room."

"Indeed? She didn't complain of a headache at dinner."

"I thought she looked a little unwell," remarked Oliphant.

"She is probably planning to go and see her friends. That should make her feel unwell," Falconer said coldly. "Have you the report for me on her friends, Oily?"

"On seven of them," Oliphant answered.

"Are they satisfactory?"

"Those seven? Wholly."

"What of the others?"

"Well, there is a young man named Judd. She sees a good deal of him," Oliphant said. "But I know very little about him - only that he has a small antique shop in Hampstead and appears to be doing well."

"*Indeed,*" said Falconer heavily.

Oliphant gave a small, almost plummy smile.

"I shouldn't assume that he is using Christine in the hope of doing business with you," he said.

"That is *exactly* what I fear he may be doing. Have you tried to find out his background?"

"Yes," said Oliphant.

"It's not like you to admit failure."

"I haven't admitted failure yet," Oliphant retorted. "I have asked Alec Hobbs if he can make some inquiries, and he will be in touch with me tomorrow."

Falconer nodded, seeming reasonably well satisfied.

"How *is* Alec?" asked Charlotte Falconer, as if hoping to change the subject. "He was so distressed by poor Helen's death. I really wondered whether he would ever get over it." After a pause, and while she poured coffee, she went on: "I could never understand why Alec elected to become a policeman."

"Some people would call him a detective," Oliphant replied.

"Is there any difference?" asked Charlotte indifferently, looking at her husband. "Richard, will you have brandy or a liqueur?"

"Brandy," answered her husband. "Brandy."

Deputy Commander Alex Hobbs, Gideon's deputy and chief assistant at Scotland Yard, sat back in an easy chair reading an American police manual, storing much of what he read in his card-index file of a mind, and half listening to *Swan Lake* on a stereo record player. He could hear cars passing along the Embankment in front of Ayling Crescent, and now and again a heavy lorry changed gear as it turned to go over Chelsea Bridge. Very occasionally a tug or a lighter hooted on the river.

There had been a time, even as recently as six or seven months before, when he would have been troubled and restless, still fighting the loneliness which had followed the death of his wife. During her long illness, they had lived in a flat not a quarter of a mile away, overlooking the same stretch of river, and her last awareness, as she lay propped up on pillows in a bed close to the window, had been of the river. When she died, Hobbs's immediate inclination had been to get completely away from this all too familiar part of London but eventually he had settled on a small suite of rooms in a modern block of flats in Chelsea. Pleasantly though somewhat severely furnished, it provided excellent service; he had nothing to worry about but getting his evening meal; and he could, whenever so minded, leave the washing up to the maid in the morning.

He would have given up, almost certainly, but for the slow growing of his interest in Gideon's daughter

Penelope. He was falling in love with her; and the Gideons knew it. But Penelope was so young, and so full of enthusiasm for younger men...

He finished a chapter and put the book down, yawned and stretched, then looked at the brandy and the empty glass on a wine table by his side. Suddenly he placed his hands on the arms of his chair and sprang up, a very fit, very lean man of forty-five, dark-haired, handsome in an almost artificial way.

He turned to the window.

Here again he had forced himself to overcome an impulse to draw the curtains every night. Helen had liked them open, and when she held been well - and even during her illness when she had been able to stand - they had often put the lights out and gone to look at the view, the Embankment and the bridges, the luminosity of the smoke pouring out of the squat chimney stacks of the Battersea Power Station, the coloured lights of the Fun Fair at Battersea Park, the slow, smooth-moving lights on the river craft. The view hadn't changed. The awareness of being alone strengthened noticeably, and he made himself stand rigidly there.

Slowly, remembered grief and present tension eased, and he relaxed.

As he did so, his telephone bell rang.

Moving toward the table where the telephone stood, within

hand's reach of his chair, he glanced at a clock standing on a bookcase which lined one wall to waist height. It was quarter to ten, late for a call from the Yard unless it was an emergency. He picked up the receiver.

"Alex Hobbs speaking."

"Good evening, sir," a man said, with a slight North Country accent which Hobbs immediately recognized. "Thwaites here, sir - sorry to bother you so late."

Whatever else, this was no emergency.

"That's all right," Hobbs said. "What is it?"

"You asked me to make inquiries about a Lancelot Judd, an antique dealer of Hampstead."

"Yes," said Hobbs.

"I would like to discuss the situation with you, sir."

"Tonight?"

"I have a full day planned tomorrow, and to do it then I'd have to put off several cases, but of course if you—"

"All right, Thwaites," Hobbs interrupted. "Come to me here, will you? Have you eaten?"

"Oh, yes, sir!"

"Good," Hobbs said. "Where are you now?"

"In Hampstead Village, sir. I'll be about half an hour."

"Right," Hobbs said. "Have you been here before?"

"No, but I know where your flat is, sir."

"Press my downstairs bell and take the lift to the fifth floor," Hobbs told him. "I'll be at the flat door to meet you."

He put down the receiver and stepped back to the window. In some ways a more incisive man than Gideon, he had acquired a surprising number of Gideon's methods and Gideon's attitudes. In fact, although they came from vastly different backgrounds, they thought in much the same way. That was why Gideon had recommended Hobbs as his deputy. Hobbs, one of the public-school policemen, came of a family which had been both rich and esteemed three hundred years ago. He had been to Repton and King's College, Cambridge, and while some thought him aloof, even snobbish, all agreed that he was a first class policeman. Now he thought over everything he had told Thwaites to do and what he knew of the Chief Inspector. Thwaites had had a North Country upbringing, followed by twenty years at the Yard; at forty-four or five, he was a rather untidy, comfortable looking man, who had acquired a love and deep knowledge of antiques.

"Always liked to poke around second hand shops when I was a boy, sir."

And he still enjoyed poking around, Hobbs believed; even when he was inquiring into an art theft, looking for stolen goods, getting information about others to be shipped out of the country, Thwaites enjoyed touching, looking at, and assessing the value of every kind of antique, painting, and *objet d'art*.

Also he was a dedicated policeman.

It was disturbing that he wanted to talk about Judd, for it suggested that all was not straightforward. Was it possible that Lord Falconer's daughter was involved with a suspicious character?

5: Rumours

"Brandy?" asked Hobbs as his visitor sat down.

"If it's all the same to you, sir, I'd rather have a beer."

Hobbs selected one of several bottles from a tray, poured it into a pewter tankard, poured a little brandy into a large-bowled glass for himself, and sat down.

"Cheers."

"Cheers." Thwaites drank, Hobbs sipped. "Well, you'll want to know what I'm making a mystery about, sir," Thwaites said. "And it *is* a bit of a mystery. This Lancelot Judd is about twenty-five, comes from Brighton, quite respectable family. He got a place at Trinity College, Oxford, read History and Philosophy and got his M.A. all right. His parents couldn't afford to do much, and he worked during the holidays at an antique shop in Brighton. He's a Peace Marcher and C.N.D. man, but otherwise he's not known. I checked with Brighton about the place where he worked. No evidence of crime or excesses of any kind."

"So he's in the clear, except for political interests," Hobbs remarked.

"That's the tricky part I wanted to talk about," Thwaites said. "*He's* in the clear, but some of the people he runs around with are"—he hesitated—"well, sir, they're what you might call on the fringe." "Fringe of what?" demanded Hobbs.

"They pick stuff up at second hand shops and markets and pass it on to the better dealers. One or two of them are believed to have handled stolen goods, although there's never been any proof. And there's one thing that sent all my warning signals going off at the same time, sir."

"What was that?" asked Hobbs.

"Judd's present girl friend is Christine Falconer, only daughter of Sir Richard Falconer. How about *that,* sir?"

Hobbs put his head on one side, eyebrows raised, and then broke into a chuckle.

"All right, you've scored," he conceded. "That's why I wanted you to check Judd."

"I did wonder, sir," said Thwaites, and drank the rest of his beer. "It *could* be young love, of course. Or it could be that he'd like to get inside the Falconers' house and see what kind of security there is - and maybe leave the odd window unfastened. Does Sir Richard suspect something like that, sir?"

"I think he's aware of the possibility."

"Can't say I blame him! Do you know what the security *is* like, sir? I've never been inside the place but Mr. Frobisher has, and he says it's like a museum."

"And it is." Hobbs got up, took Thwaites's tankard and refilled it, and sat down again. "Have you talked to the Divisional men at Hampstead?"

"Yes, sir."

"Got anything?"

"No, I don't think so," answered Thwaites. "Only rumours."

"What kind of rumours?"

"That there's a big buyer around town."

"Buyer of stolen antiques, you mean?"

"Buyer of anything at the right price," answered Thwaites. "And the rumour isn't only in Hampstead, either. It's in Chelsea and Fulham and the West End - that antique supermarket, as they call it - as well as the suburbs. And I had a word with Brighton, as I said, and Salisbury and Stratford-on-Avon. The word's out that there's a big buyer on the lookout for anything special in pictures and antiques, and that he doesn't care where it comes from - will ask no questions, in other words."

Hobbs, brandy glass cupped in both hands, sniffed at the

bouquet and looked thoughtfully at Thwaites over the brim. Apart from the noises outside and Thwaites's rather heavy breathing, there was no sound. At last, he lowered the glass.

"Do you know anyone behind it?"

"Not a soul," said Thwaites.

"Who spread the rumours? Do you know that?"

"The runners, as usual."

"No one runner in particular?" asked Hobbs.

"Haven't been able to put a finger on any one, sir. It seems to have started a week ago, and just spread. And the Falconer place could be very vulnerable. Prevention's better than cure," Thwaites added sententiously.

Hobbs sniffed brandy again, pausing as if he wanted the fumes to go through his head and clear his mind before making any comments. Then: "What are you doing?"

"I've asked the reliable dealers to pass on any word they get, but that's not good enough by itself, of course."

"It certainly isn't. Any ideas?"

"I can't say I have, sir. Except—"

"Well?" Hobbs knew the other was waiting to be prompted, and also knew how very shrewd this slow-speaking man was.

"I thought we might pick up one or two runners and pay them enough to keep them loyal," Thwaites suggested. "Someone who would pass any word on to us without letting us down. See what I mean, sir?"

"It's hardly original," Hobbs said, almost disparagingly. *"Can we rely on any runners?"*

"One, for certain," Thwaites said. "And two or three others I think would be all right."

"Can we afford to take a chance?" asked Hobbs.

"Don't see why not," said Thwaites. "And we could compare the different reports. If there's a common factor, we'd soon find out. The only risk is that the runners might reveal that they were working for us, but that wouldn't matter, as we wouldn't ask them to look for anything specific. I wondered if you would think it over and, if you agree it's worthwhile, have a word with the Commander."

"I'll do that anyhow," Hobbs said. "Who is the one runner you think we can rely on?"

"Man named Red Thomas," answered Thwaites, without hesitation. "He's always absolutely clean, though he's always in need of money. No one likes him but everyone trusts him."

"Why doesn't he have any money?" asked Hobbs.

"Spends what he gets too freely," Thwaites said with a grimace. "If you agree, sir, the first place I'd send him would be to Hampstead. The more I think about this Lancelot Judd and Christine Falconer, the more I think Hampstead's a place to concentrate on."

"I'll talk to Mr. Gideon in the morning," Hobbs said.

Gideon listened with his customary close attention next morning, and came to a conclusion more quickly than usual. It was almost as if he had been pondering most of the night, as Hobbs had been.

"Give Thwaites his head," he ordered. "I'll support him if anything goes wrong."

"Good," said Hobbs.

"And Alec - keep me in close touch," Gideon warned.

"I will," promised Hobbs. "If there is a big buyer, we want to know who he is and whether he's been buying

for long."

"We need to know that very much," Gideon said. He nodded dismissal and Hobbs went to his smaller room next door, but before he could have settled at his desk Gideon lifted the interoffice telephone on his desk and dialled him. "Alec," he said as soon as he heard the other lift the receiver, "this is worth a teletype inquiry to New York and Paris, and anywhere else abroad that might have some information for us. See to it, will you?"

"At once," said Hobbs.

"I'll see what I can do, Mr. Thwaites," Red Thomas promised.

It was the day after his visit to Lucy Jenkins, and the same time that Gideon was talking to Hobbs at the Yard. "I haven't heard anything yet, but that means nothing, as I haven't been listening. I keep myself to myself, you know that. I'll phone you whenever I get anything, Mr. Thwaites."

"Between nine o'clock and ten in the morning is best," Thwaites told him. "Here's a fiver in advance. For every reliable piece of information, you'll get another one, and a bonus if there's anything we can act on."

Red took the five-pound note with the same alacrity as he had taken the two notes from Mrs. Bessell, backed a few steps, then went out of the Chelsea Divisional Station, where he and Thwaites had met. Once outside, he walked very quickly toward King's Road, as if he could not get away quickly enough. Traffic was thick and there was a line of five buses outside the Town Hall. Red jumped onto the first of these and sat on the edge of a seat close to the platform. A Jamaican conductress took the sixpence he offered, and he accepted the ticket which rolled out of her machine, without a word. When he got off, on the far side of Albert Bridge, he walked toward Fisk's shop.

On the other side of the road was a young policeman, one of the two who had seen him the previous day.

Lucy Jenkins was in the shop, using a damp chamois over some china pieces. She looked up, and the moment she recognized him, her features froze.

"The old man in?" he demanded.

"No, he's out again," she said, almost vindictively.

"No wonder he never does any business, he's always out," complained Red.

"That's *his* business," she retorted.

"All right, all right. I want to look at those pictures again."

"Look where you like," she said carelessly.

Thomas went across to the pictures leaning up against the wall, and began to play the familiar game. It was silly, really, because all the runners did it. He went through picture after picture and pretended not to be interested in any but lingered over several. She began to play her usual game of guessing which ones interested him. The pheasants, she decided, and was immediately worried because they *were* the best among the pictures and she could not knock much off the asking price. The old man had told her the limits.

Red selected a picture - yes, it was one of the pheasants.

"How much?" he asked.

"It's on the label."

"I don't take any notice of the label," he said. "How much to the trade, I mean."

Lucy went across to him and took the picture out of his hands, looked at the back, and saw the freshly attached label: "£30 pr."

"Thirty pounds the pair," she said.

"Who asked for the pair?"

"Whoever buys them will get the pair," she insisted.

"When's he coming back?" demanded Red.

"He might come in any time, but might be out all day" she countered.

"If he finds out you've missed a sale, you'll be in for it," he warned.

"Who's going to tell him?"

"I am."

"Think he'll believe you?" she scoffed. "That'll be the day!"

"Stop arguing around, Lucy," Red Thomas urged in a more reasoning voice. "How much?" His tone and manner changed and Lucy knew that he had finished the game and was playing it straight. He must have a customer or he wouldn't be so serious, and every pound she knocked off would be one in his pocket, for if she knew the man he had seen the price yesterday and quoted it - perhaps higher - to his customer.

"Twenty-seven ten the pair," she said.

"Twenty-five."

"Twenty-seven, and I may have to make the ten bob up myself."

He looked at her for a long time, without making comment

or retort, and then when she was beginning to feel uneasy under his gaze, he said: "Twenty now, seven when I've been paid."

"Who's buying?"

"That's my secret," he said. "Is it a deal?"

"Oh, all right," she conceded ungraciously. "Give me the twenty and be back before Mr. Fisk comes in or I'll be in trouble."

"No, you won't," Red said. "I never cheated anyone yet, and you know it."

She did know it. She knew also that if a runner ever welshed he would be out of the game for good. One could put a lot of profit onto the price paid, but one couldn't welsh or play one customer or buyer off against another. It was an absolute rule, and the trade lived by it.

He took some notes out of his pocket and counted twenty of them into her hands; he had one left when he was done. She gave him a receipt and he looked round, found some corrugated paper, wrapped the pictures up, fastened the paper with sealing tape, and went out.

Nearly an hour later, he was with Mrs. Bessell in the Bond Street gallery, watching her as she studied the pictures, first with the naked eye and then through a magnifying glass. He was trembling a little. At last, she put them down and said: "How much did you have to pay for them?"

"Twenty-seven ten."

"Where did you get them from?" Mrs. Bessell's manner was uncompromising.

He hesitated before saying: "Jake Fisk. I told you."

"Any idea where *he* got them?"

"No," said Red. "Why—they're not hot, are they?"

"I don't think so," she said. "They're probably early Stott, and if they're not they're a very good example of the school. They're worth two or three hundred apiece, anyhow."

"Gawd!"

"Red," she asked, "has Fisk got any more? If he has, can you put all his stock on approval, and let me have a look? If you can do that, I'll give you a hundred for this pair. I know where I can place them, and I could place plenty more."

"I'll find out," Red promised, breathing very hard. "That's what I'll do, I'll find out pretty damned quick."

It did not occur to his strangely literal mind that when she talked of hundreds she could mean thousands.

He went out and hurried in his usual nervous way along Bond Street, and as he stood waiting for the lights to change at Piccadilly, he saw a man whom he recognized, another runner, named Slater. Slater was walking toward Piccadilly Circus and making surprising speed on his short, fat legs. There was a great intentness about him, Red noticed.

"He's onto a good thing," he told himself. "He can't have been to. Old Fisk's, can he?"

Apprehensive lest Slater had forestalled him, Red rushed across the road to catch a bus, while Slater walked toward a bus stop outside the Royal Academy, heading for Trafalgar Square and the National Gallery.

It was half past ten.

At eleven o'clock, they were to begin the raid on the National Gallery.

6: The Theft

The steps leading up to the National Gallery were thronged with children in their early teens, a mixed bag of sexes and sizes, white and black, English, Indian, Pakistani and Jamaican - all awaiting the orders of their teachers who were to guide them round the gallery but who were now inside, seeing to the formalities. Some of the youngsters watched the traffic and the people, the thronged square, the flocks of pigeons and the dozens who fed them, the clicking cameras as pigeons that perched on hands and shoulders and heads were photographed for family posterity.

Slater got off his bus opposite the south side of St. Martin-in-the-Fields and walked to the National Gallery. He kept looking about him, half fearful of seeing someone he knew. A young policeman was walking along the pavement, controlling a crowd of French youths waiting to go in. His back was toward Slater.

Leslie Jenkins came out, and he and Slater passed each other with raised eyebrows; that was the signal; so all was well, and Jenkins had made the first cut in the picture to be stolen.

Slater went inside. It was shadowy and noises were subdued.

Slater turned right, then left, knowing exactly where to go but looking casually at each picture, noticing the groups in front of some, the tired and the old on the small couches, the attendants who stood with what seemed all-seeing patience in the doorways. Now and again, a voice was raised, often an

American's; one man, harsh and guttural, could be heard above the rest whenever he spoke.

Slater reached a Velazquez, the portrait of a young man, rich in colours; the youth's dress seemed to be actual silk and velvet, his face actual flesh.

Two people stood in front of it, studying it in detail; others looked at it from a distance. A small crowd sauntered in and a guide began to talk. The words "Spanish school . . . seventeenth century . . . early period of harmony . . . Court Painter to the Court of Spain . . ." filtered through the subdued hum of conversation and shuffling feet.

Slater heard all this yet was oblivious.

A couple came in and went closer to the portrait, one stretching out a hand as if to touch it; the other said something that made him draw back. A man with a magnifying glass went very close, obviously studying the jewels on the young man's hand - the pearls seemed to be objects one could pluck from the canvas, the diamonds to need only a little extra light to make them scintillate.

Slater went out of this room, but soon came back - exactly as planned. He stayed with a group some distance from the Velazquez until he saw two women approach the attendant. Then he moved forward, hand out-stretched, much as others had done. There was no one nearby.

He pierced the canvas, and his heart leapt.

He cut, and his heart raced.

He stood back, as if admiring, and he felt a quiver of nausea.

He mixed with the crowd, still standing and studying, saw the attendant glance at him and glance away. After a while, he went out again, sauntering, calmer. No one took any notice of him.

On his way, he passed Leslie Jenkins, and he recognized him though he wore a light raincoat and looked very different with a beard, dark and heavy at the chin but curly and fluffy at the cheeks.

A few minutes later, de Courvier entered the gallery.

The scene was almost identical with that which he and his fellow plotters had foreseen. He needed a little more time, that was all, and he had planned for it without saying a word to the others. As he stood looking at the painting, a long-legged girl obviously not English approached the attendant and spoke excitedly in French.

"I have lost my handbag; have you found it here, please?"

Every head turned at the attractive voice.

"No, Miss, I-"

"But I have lost it! All my money is in the bag and I am sure I left it in this room." She spun round, very lovely to look at, and pointed at a couch where four elderly women and a young man sat, looking suddenly embarrassed, almost as if they were guilty. The girl pointed. "It was there, I tell you!"

"I haven't seen it, Miss," the attendant insisted, "but I'll have a look." He walked toward the couch and even those who pretended not to be looking at the scene were distracted; only de Courvier, studying the Velazquez intently, seemed to be absorbed in what he was doing.

He *was* absorbed.

He pierced and cut and pulled the canvas free, then let it coil beneath his coat as he placed the copy in position. It was masterly sleight of hand; no one who was not intent on every movement he made could possibly have suspected what he had done.

He walked without haste toward the next room.

The French girl cried in sudden delight: *"It is there!"*

The youth who had been sitting on the couch shifted to one side. There was a small, flat handbag pushed between the seat and the back of the couch.

The attendant, highly gratified, said, "I knew I hadn't seen it."

"Oh, I am so pleased!"

"Better look inside to make sure everything is in it," the attendant advised.

"Yes, I will." There was a tense pause as she opened the bag under the fascinated gaze of everyone present, drew out a wallet, then a passport, talking excitedly all the time. "Money . . . passport . . . my air ticket to Paris . . . ticket for the theatre tonight . . . I have everything!"

"*Very* glad it turned out all right, Miss." The man spoke as if this happy outcome was due wholly to him.

There were murmurs of pleasure, congratulations, and relief. The girl went out, the men's gaze following her beautiful legs. The whole atmosphere seemed brighter; there was a buzz of talk, and a crocodile of schoolchildren suddenly appeared.

Outside, de Courvier hailed a taxi, was taken to where his car was parked, at the underground garage beneath Hyde Park. He walked from the spot where the taxi dropped him, and got into his car, a blue Jaguar two and-a-half litre. Taking the rolled canvas from his coat, he wrapped it in a piece of new canvas from the back of the car. Then he lit a cigarette and sat back; for the first time, he was perspiring and showing signs of strain.

A Morris 1100 appeared, shiny red, two youths in the front seat. Neither of them waved to him but each looked his way. A few minutes later, they approached him as he sat waiting in his car. No one else was in sight but in another section of the garage a car started up.

The young men came to de Courvier from either side as he wound down the driving window.

"Got it?" asked one of the youths.

"Yes."

"Let's see."

De Courvier opened the roll enough for them to see the face, and one of them leaned inside and shone a torch brightly onto a corner. He clicked the torch off.

"Okay."

"Now let me see the money," de Courvier said.

The youth who had examined the picture stood aside. The

other pushed a box through the window, heavy enough to fall painfully onto de Courvier's knees; he was obviously eager and excited and there was something fresh and even pleasant about his grin. "Don't lose it," he said.

"I won't lose it. Do you want anything else?"

"We'll let you know," the youth said, and he turned away.

De Courvier put a hand on the box, and then lit another cigarette. He was trembling from the reaction, and felt almost suffocated; he must get some air. Once he started the engine, he felt calmer, and he drove slowly from the garage, paid the exit fee, went up into Hyde Park, and drove on the inside lane toward the Marble Arch and Bayswater. He stayed inside the park, still driving slowly, until he neared the Serpentine. It was a grey day and there were fewer people than usual; he had room to park. He smoked two more cigarettes, and then opened the box with great care.

The top bundle was of a hundred ten-pound notes; a thousand pounds.

The next was of a hundred one-hundred-dollar bills; four thousand pounds.

De Courvier closed the box and drove off.

"Twenty-four thousand in all," he said to the others when they met at his flat in Hampstead. "Eight thousand each, half in dollars, half in pounds. We'll get the rest when the picture's been checked and authenticated. Split it up, keep it safe, and don't start spending too freely. We do not wish to attract attention at this time."

Slater said, in a hoarse voice, "I'm going to have a holiday. I'm going to Brighton on holiday, that's me."

"What about you?" de Courvier asked Jenkins.

"I'm going to stay home," Jenkins said. "I'm going to count the dough, that's all I'm going to do. *Count the* dough."

Later, when Jenkins reached his little terrace house where the three had met to plot this crime, the first thing he did was to make himself some tea. Then he drew the flimsy curtains at the window, pulled up a chair near the one in which he had been sitting, and placed bundles of currency notes on the chair. He drank tea, and gloated; began to doze, and was in a state of euphoria, beautifully tired, gloriously, sensuously pleased with life.

He went to sleep.

While he was sleeping a long-legged girl wearing stretch pants and carrying a shoulder satchel quietly let herself into the house with a key. She drew on a pair of flimsy nylon gloves, collected the notes and placed them in the satchel, and slung it back over her shoulder. She stood looking at the sleeping man, a strangely tense expression on her face. Suddenly, she moved silently toward the gas fire, turned off the gas, let the mantles get cool, then turned on the gas again. Then she went to the meter, near the sink, and put in ten separate shillings.

Throughout all this, Jenkins had not stirred.

Slater reached Brighton Station early that evening, and walked toward the sea front. Since he was used to walking, in spite of his weight, it was not too long before he reached the promenade and the main pier, near the aquarium. Every now and again, he fondled the suitcase he carried, and most of the time he wore a fatuous grin.

He did not notice that he was followed by a slim youth wearing corduroys and an olive-green jacket.

At last, he went across the road, and walked until he found a hotel of a much better class than he could usually afford. He asked for a room overlooking the sea and when he was in the room, opened his case, removed a clean shirt and some underclothes, and then the packets of pounds and dollars. He spread them over the bed with great deliberation, stood beaming for a long time, and then almost reluctantly stepped to the window and looked out. The sea was grey but absolutely calm. A few rowing boats were moving sluggishly, young men at the oars. The crunching of people walking over the pebbles came clearly and regularly, and there was a little *hiss-siss-siss* of sound of the tide running on the pebbles and then slowly seeping back.

He heard footsteps, and almost at once there was a tap at the door. In sudden panic, he cried, "Just a minute!" He sprang to the bed and pulled the bedspread down from the pillow, covering the notes. Putting the suitcase on the foot of the bed, he belatedly called out, "Who is it?"

"It's the manager," a man called. "I'm sorry, sir, butI forgot your registration form."

Slater, heart still thumping but not even slightly suspicious, went across and unlocked and opened the door.

A young man in olive green simply drove a long bladed knife into his belly.

The crowds went to and fro along the passages of the National Gallery; hundreds of people stood in front of the Velazquez, but no one appeared to suspect that anything at all was wrong.

7: The News Breaks

At half past nine the next morning, Gideon entered his office at the Yard, and the day's routine began. It had altered a little since Hobbs had become his deputy, virtually replacing Chief Superintendent Lemaitre, an old friend as well as assistant. Lemaitre was now in charge of a division, probably the job in which he was happiest, but certain mornings Gideon missed him. This was one of the mornings, and he could not even begin to think why. He sat at his big pedestal desk, where there were several trays: "IN," "OUT," "PENDING," "URGENT," "ASSISTANT COMMISSIONER", and, centred on the desk, the files on cases which needed reviewing that morning.

At one time, Gideon would have seen all the Superintendents and Chief Inspectors in charge of these cases, but nowadays Hobbs saw some of them and decided whom Gideon should interview and in what order. This was far more efficient, and freed Gideon for other work; moreover, he had come to trust Hobbs's judgment almost as much as he trusted his own. Yet it wasn't quite the same: nothing was quite the same.

There were six cases; a report from Frobisher in Manchester, about the North Country museum theft; one from Lemaitre's division, about a counterfeiting case in which someone had tried to do the work of the Mint with the new decimal coinage; the almost inevitable investigation into a hijacking case, this time one of a series of thefts of tobacco and cigarettes; the fourth to do with the smuggling of Pakistanis into England in Sussex, the kind of problem which greatly troubled Gideon.

Law or no law, he did not like to have to punish people for wanting to live in Britain, and he did not like to think that here in London there were men who were dealing in immigrants almost as heartlessly as others, not so very long ago, had dealt in slaves. He spent more time on this case than the others, but finally opened the next file, which concerned organized crime in the West End and contained reports about men and women suspected of corrupting witnesses, of using threats and menaces and sometimes physical violence to make witnesses do what they were told.

It was an ugly situation, and needed the closest possible study.

The sixth and last case could not have been more different. It was one that the Yard was reopening for its own satisfaction, for there was some reason to believe that a man serving a life sentence for murdering his wife might have been wrongly convicted.

Gideon rang for Hobbs, who appeared in the doorway between the two rooms. Hobbs was his usual composed self, just a little more like a stockbroker or a banker than a Yard man.

"Good morning, Alec."

"Good morning," Hobbs said, and then smiled faintly. "You look almost belligerent this morning."

"I've been reading the hijack business," Gideon said. "We've got to break that wide open before it gets much bigger."

"I wish we knew how big it is," said Hobbs.

"Yes." Gideon brooded. The hijacking and the immigration problem were the ones he should concentrate on, and Hobbs knew that as well as he did. He shrugged his shoulders. "Sit down," he invited, and as Hobbs sat, he asked, "Anything from Brighton about the Pakistani business?"

"Nothing new," Hobbs replied. "I thought you might want to talk about it." That was Hobbs's way of saying, "It's time you went into it more closely, George."

"But there's something else from Brighton," Hobbs said,

"and we may be asked to send someone down."

"Oh? What?"

"A man named Slater was murdered in a hotel," Hobbs told him. "As far as Brighton can find out, he opened the door to someone who knifed him, then pushed him onto the bed, covered him over, and locked the door from the outside. A maid wanted to do the room this morning, and when he didn't respond to taps on the door, she opened it with her passkey. The manager ran up when he heard her screaming. The man had been knifed through the stomach - dead for over twelve hours; *rigor* was well in."

Gideon drummed his fingers on his desk.

"Slater—Slater. I've heard the name in connection with art, haven't I?"

"The Pembroke art theft, seven years ago," Hobbs told him.

"That's it," said Gideon. "He was the van driver."

"That's the man," agreed Hobbs. "There's a rather queer thing about it, too."

"What?"

"A single hundred-dollar bill was found on the floor, just beneath the bed. On top of the dust."

Gideon said slowly, "Has Brighton asked for help?"

"Not yet."

"Who would you send?"

"Frobisher is coming back from Manchester today," Hobbs told him. "They haven't had any luck up there, and he says there doesn't seem any more that he can do."

"If Brighton does ask for help, send Frobisher," Gideon said. "I'd like a word with him before he goes." He hesitated, then lifted a receiver and asked, "Is Mr. Chamberlain in?" Chamberlain was the present Assistant Commissioner for crime, new to the post. There had been a succession of appointments to it, none of them satisfactory, and Gideon would have preferred to go straight to the Commissioner, but protocol prevented this.

"You're through to Mr. Chamberlain," the operator said.

"Good morning, sir," Gideon said formally. "There's been a murder at Brighton, and I think it would be a good thing if we were called in . . . I understand that we can't insist, of course, but in this case I think we could anticipate things a bit . . . ." There was a long pause, and Hobbs saw Gideon's expression change, saw the hard glint in his eyes. "Very good, sir," he said, and rang off.

It was a long time since Hobbs had seen Gideon look so angry, and he sat very still and silent; Gideon put his right hand in his pocket and took out a pipe with a large bowl. He had not smoked it for years, but he often smoothed the shiny bowl while it was inside his pocket. Hobbs could not recall having seen him take it out for several months; Lemaitre could have told him it was the one certain indication that Gideon was very angry indeed.

In a studiously even voice, he said, "The Assistant Commissioner doesn't want me or anyone else to suggest to Brighton that we would like to be consulted over Slater's murder. It is a matter which must be broached by Brighton to us."

Hobbs said heavily, "I see."

"Did Brighton tell you anything else?" Gideon asked, still very calm.

"No."

"Not about the smuggled-Pakistani business?"

"That's being handled mainly by Sussex," Hobbs said.

"But Brighton is involved."

"Yes."

"I want to go into the smuggling," Gideon said. "The latest report" - he put his hand on the filenames - "names three key men in London who may be organizing the racket. Are you convinced that Riddell is the best man for the job?"

Hobbs didn't answer.

"Well, are you or aren't you?" growled Gideon.

"I don't think either of us would have assigned Riddell to the job," said Hobbs. "He was the best available man when we first needed some information."

"So you're not satisfied with him," said Gideon.

"Not completely, no."

Gideon looked down at his hand, rounded into a fist with the pipe inside it, then clenched and clenched again, making the knuckles show pale against the leathery skin. He looked back at Hobbs, and was about to speak when one of the telephones rang. As if glad of the interruption, he picked up the receiver with his free hand.

"Gideon . . . Who? . . . *What?"* He almost bellowed; Hobbs had never heard him shout louder. He listened for a long time, and then went on in a quieter voice, "When? . . . Who? . . . How? . . ." He listened again, and then said, "Right." He banged down the receiver, seemed to smoulder for a long time, and then said to Hobbs, in a very different tone, "A portrait by Velazquez, valued at over two hundred thousand pounds, has been stolen from the National Gallery, presumably yesterday. Is Thwaites in?"

"He was just before I came in here." Hobbs caught his breath. "May I?" He touched the interoffice telephone and dialled. "Chief Inspectors' Room? . . . Mr. Thwaites there? . . . Yes . . . Hallo, Thwaites. Come along to Mr. Gideon's office, at once."

He put down the receiver slowly, obviously badly shaken himself. Gideon had put his pipe away, as if something of his earlier tension had left him. He was still hard-faced and gruff, but no longer spoke with studied self-control.

"Stay while I talk to Thwaites, will you? Then I needn't tell the story twice." He smiled faintly. "Seems too much for coincidence, doesn't it? An ex-convict involved in an old art theft murdered the day after another art theft." There was a brief pause before he went on. "Alec, we need to replace Riddell. Think of a man who would do a better job on this immigration business, will you?"

As he spoke, there was a tap at the door, and Thwaites entered, massive enough to fill the doorway, a little untidy, and in need of a haircut; his suit needed cleaning and pressing, too;

there were stains on the lapels and the lower part of the jacket.

Gideon was fully aware that even for an old-timer at the Yard a summons to the Commander's office could be quite an ordeal, so he raised a hand in greeting. "Come in, Thwaites. Sit down. Cigarette?" All of this gave Thwaites time to overcome any momentary qualms. Gideon pushed a box of cigarettes across the desk and Thwaites took one and lit up. "Mr. Hobbs told me yesterday about your inquiries out at Hampstead and the connection with Sir Richard Falconer."

Thwaites said, "And young Judd, sir."

"And also the talk that there is a big buyer around who will buy what he wants and ask no questions," Gideon said. "Now we've just heard of a major art theft that is going to cause us a lot of trouble unless we can do a quick job on it."

Thwaites's nervousness vanished in the instant.

"Something for me, sir?"

"Yes," Gideon said, and went on with great deliberation: "The Velazquez 'Prince' has been stolen from the National Gallery."

Thwaites, already leaning forward on his chair, sat perched with one hand stretched out as if fending off danger, his lips parted, showing very crowded but very white teeth in his lower jaw. He had a heavy jowl and a slightly bloodhound look, and his greying hair was thinning to a large bald patch. It was as if he had been struck dumb; even his breath seemed to stop.

Both Gideon and Hobbs watched, fascinated.

Gradually, Thwaites came to life, breathing inward slowly and then exuding a long, deep breath as he settled slowly back in his chair.

"How the hell did they do it?" he demanded gustily.

"That's what you're to find out," Gideon told him. "No one yet knows when it was done, but it was either during the night or early this morning. They open to the public at ten o'clock; a woman artist is making a copy of 'The Prince' and can't work when crowds are about, so she comes in before the gallery opens and after it closes. She was later than usual this morning - arrived about nine o'clock. She put up her easel and got her paints out, then studied the hand, which she was painting yesterday. Apparently, she knew at a glance that the texture was different, and when she took a close look, she raised the alarm. The Director was away, but the Acting Keeper was told the moment he got in. He telephoned me." For the first time, Gideon paused, only to ask, "What help do you need, Thwaites?"

Thwaites hesitated, pursing his lips.

"You can have as many men as you want," Gideon said. "This is going to cause a sensation, and we don't want another fuss like the one we had over 'The Duke of Wellington.' "

"I wasn't really thinking of what help I would need," said Thwaites, and he seemed a little embarrassed. "Excuse me, sir, but isn't this much more Mr. Frobisher's job?"

"He won't be back until mid-afternoon," Gideon said.

Thwaites raised his arms from his side, then let them flop in a gesture of resignation, and he looked as doleful as the bloodhound he resembled when he said: "Then I'd like six or seven men, sir, and a full team of experts. I'd like to treat this as seriously as a murder investigation."

"Right!" Gideon pushed his chair back in a gesture of dismissal. "Mr. Hobbs will see you get what you want. You get over to the National Gallery as soon as you can, and—"

"Excuse me, sir," Thwaites interrupted, with a kind of gloomy daring, "but would you go over yourself? Or ask Mr. Hobbs—?" He broke off, confused and yet doggedly persistent, glancing at Hobbs with a no offence-intended expression in his brown eyes. "I think it would be wise if one of you did."

"All right," Gideon said. "How long will you need to get your team ready and be over there?"

"Should be able to do it comfortably in half an hour, sir."

"Good. Ask for Mr. Peebles, the Acting Keeper. One of us will be with him by the time you get there," Gideon said.

"Thank you very much indeed," said Thwaites, obviously

greatly relieved.

Gideon also felt a sense of relief, a sense almost of pleasure, and as Thwaites went out he remembered the cold rage that had surged within when the Assistant Commissioner had spoken to him as if he were a cadet not yet out of training. He still felt resentment but no longer needed to exert himself to control his mood, and he welcomed the idea of going to the National Gallery himself.

Hobbs was speaking into the telephone.

"Send a car round at once for the Commander." He put down the receiver and asked, "You going, sir, or shall I?"

"I'll go," said Gideon. At once he was doubtful, seeing an expression in Hobbs's eyes which he read as disagreement or disapproval. He thought a little more swiftly than he spoke. "Thwaites seems to think that the National Gallery officials will prefer to deal with some top brass to begin with. Do you know anyone over there?"

"I know the Director, but he's out of the country," Hobbs answered. "In Italy, I believe, studying the way they've restored some of the paintings after the flood at the Pitti Palace." He paused a moment, then continued, "One thing Thwaites ought to be told, if he thinks he's going to be out of his depth socially or intellectually." Ah.

"What?" asked Gideon, almost ominously.

"Not to be a bloody fool," said Hobbs. "They're not interested in the old-school tie; all they need to be sure of is that he knows what he's talking about and doesn't look on 'The Prince' as a bundle of banknotes."

"Oh," said Gideon, completely taken aback. But it wasn't long before he began to smile. Then he chuckled. "Good!" he said heartily. "I'll make sure they know what he's like; you brief him." He pushed his chair right back, stood up, and was at the door when he stopped to turn round. "This Pakistani immigration business."

"Yes?" said Hobbs.

"Any idea who'd be right to replace Riddell?"

"Yes," answered Hobbs promptly. "I'd like Honiwell if he weren't on the Entwhistle case. He'd have to be fairly mobile for the immigration inquiry, which might make it difficult for him, to do both."

"We'll think about it," said Gideon.

"We'll think about it," Hobbs repeated to himself when he was alone in his own office. His set expression, which so often gave him a look of arrogance, eased into a smile and the expression in his eyes was warm. "The day will come when he really will accept me." Rather in the manner of Gideon, he chuckled; then he picked up the telephone to speak to Thwaites.

8: The Whispers

As Gideon stepped into the car that was waiting for him at the foot of the Yard's steps, Big Ben struck eleven o'clock, the notes booming out sonorously and with doom-like inevitability. Beneath and around the tower, London's traffic surged in its unending variety, and a few Members of Parliament, there for early work in committee, drove into the courtyard of the House of Commons. A group of late-season American tourists were looking, perhaps with disbelief, at the statue of Abraham Lincoln: the man who had best defined democracy keeping a silent watch on a citadel of democracy which was so often besieged with invisible enemies. There were sightseers in Whitehall, too, the usual groups about the statue-like Horse Guards, sabres drawn and helmets shimmering. As Gideon passed, he saw a gawky child reach up and touch a horse's nose.

The traffic lights favoured Gideon, and his car swept across Trafalgar Square and then to the National Gallery. There crowds of people milled about the pavement and up the steps. On the steps themselves and at the entrance were thicker crowds, and as Gideon stepped out he heard plaintive calls and protesting and some strident voices.

"Why don't they open the doors?"

"They won't let us in, that's the trouble."

Policemen, keeping order and preventing the crowd from surging onto the road, saw and recognized Gideon. One saluted.

"Good morning, sir."

"Morning. Clear a path, will you?"

"Yes, sir." The constable had a hawkish face but a soft voice. With a kind of terrier patience, he forged a path through the crowd, and as Gideon stepped onto the big porch, he saw three other policemen guarding the doors, while a youth who had come up the staircase on the other side called: "Mr. Gideon!"

Gideon looked up - and a camera flashed.

"Excuse me, Commander," an older man called out, "but what's happened?"

Someone else began, "There a rumour that the—"

"As soon as anything's known for certain, there will be a statement," Gideon assured them. He pushed past the doorway and into the near-deserted hall, the South Vestibule. Here at the entrance turnstiles and the sales counters, assistants stood about aimlessly; two men on duty at the cloakroom, ready to collect cameras and umbrellas as well as hats and coats, looked baffled.

Gideon was thinking, If we don't get the place open soon, we'll have half Fleet Street here.

A tall man wearing a velvet suit, tight-waisted and looking vaguely old-fashioned, with a floppy bow tie and long but well-groomed hair, came forward.

"Commander Gideon, how very good of you to come in person." The man stretched out his hand. "I am David Morcom, the Assistant Keeper." His hand looked pale, the skin and flesh almost translucent, and Gideon was prepared to grip momentarily but not too firmly.

But Morcom's fingers bit into his hand like steel wire.

"My men are on the way over," Gideon said. "I came to see if there's any immediate thing I can do. We don't want another Goya affair."

"My God, we don't!" exclaimed Morcom. He gave an unexpectedly charming smile. "The one reassurance I needed was that this would have the most urgent attention, and I don't need any more telling. Would you like to see the room the picture was stolen from?"

"Yes," Gideon said, "I certainly would."

"We'll go along here," said Morcom. "Oh, Commander. I have to make a decision very quickly about opening this morning. You've seen for yourself what a crowd there is outside. What do you think I should do?"

"Give me a little time to think that over," Gideon said.

They were walking, Morcom with very spritely step, Gideon with his customary deliberateness, along the galleries to the right, past attendants standing in little groups talking. All of them stopped at sight of the two men, and two or three times a whisper floated after them.

"That's Gideon."

"That's the Commander himself."

"That's Gideon—Gideon—Gideon—"

It was like an echo, growing fainter and fainter.

Gideon, though used to finding his way about unfamiliar places, tried but failed to keep track of the different rooms they entered. Why did every picture gallery and museum seem like a maze? He found himself thinking of a man plotting a theft here. It would be so easy to disappear from one room and virtually vanish. If the man had an accomplice who slipped him a raincoat, say, or a cap, or if he had either one concealed underneath his jacket, he would be able to confuse all descriptions of him. But this was no moment to ask what the security precautions of the museum were, and in any case Thwaites was the man to check that. Frobisher certainly knew, of course. Whatever they were, the actual layout of the building would make a getaway comparatively easy.

They entered a small room - XLJ, Gideon noticed. There were more attendants here than in any of the other rooms, and two men who were obviously senior in rank. In front of a picture now cordoned off was a frail-looking, grey-haired woman with an easel by her side, sitting on a canvas folding chair.

Morcom went straight up to her.

"I'm sorry to have to keep you, Mrs. Templeton, and it won't be a moment longer than I can help. The police experts are on their way. This is Commander Gideon."

Mrs. Templeton got up with surprising agility.

"I've heard of you, of course," she said, in a deep pleasant voice. "And you mustn't worry about how long you need me, Mr. Gideon. I have nothing to do, and to tell you the truth this is quite exciting." She smiled at him. "Is that very wicked?"

"Very," Gideon replied dryly, and her eyes had laughter in them. "I've heard what a help you've been. If you hadn't been so quick to notice something wrong, Mr. Morcom might have been much longer realizing the picture had been substituted." He moved a little closer to the one in the frame. "Would you call it a good copy?"

"I've seen a lot worse," said Mrs. Templeton.

"Unless it was scrutinized closely, most of the gallery staff would have been fooled," Morcom interpolated.

"Is it possible to say who made the copy?" asked Gideon.

Morcom nodded. "I think so. We keep records of anyone who's had permission to do one - they should be quite comprehensive."

"I think you'll find it's by Totter, and was done fifty years ago," said Mrs. Templeton. "I saw it for sale in Paignton, I think it was, about seven years ago."

"That's very useful information." Gideon looked at the woman appreciatively, then turned to Morcom. "Let Chief Inspector Thwaites know, will you? If we can find who owned or bought it lately, it will be a great help. How was the job done? Do you know that yet?"

"Cut from the frame, obviously with a special instrument, possibly a diamond-edged cutter," answered Morcom. "The whole thing must have been done in a matter of seconds. It was almost like sleight of hand." He sounded exasperated.

"Sleight of hand," Gideon echoed. "Were you here yesterday, Mrs. Templeton?"

"In the morning, yes, until a little after ten o'clock. And, yes"

- her youthful and alert eyes twinkled again - "the genuine Velazquez *was* here then, beyond any possible doubt. You see, I was painting the left hand, and the thumb is slightly deformed - wrinkled, perhaps I should say. I was trying to copy it, but I fell very far short, and yesterday morning I worked on in the hope of catching just the right mood. I couldn't. I gave up in despair and told myself that it wasn't worth spending time on. That's why I didn't come last night. But this morning I simply had to try again, and I brought a special glass." She picked a small magnifying glass up from the easel. "I thought if I could enlarge it I might be able to come near, but—it simply isn't the same thumb."

"Excuse me, sir," one of the men standing by said.

Morcom glanced up at him.

"Yes? Oh, Commander, this is our head security officer, Mr. Gordon Smith."

Gideon nodded.

Smith said mechanically, "Glad to know you, sir," and then went on: "Mrs. Templeton told us about this and I sent for the Fortuna Press book of Velazquez; we have some in stock. It shows the thumb very clearly, sir." He moved to a couch in the centre of the room and picked up a heavy book with an illustration of Velazquez's dwarfs on the front. "Would you care to look, sir?" He opened the book, which he had to support on both arms.

"Good idea," Morcom said. "Thank you." They all peered at the full-page plate of 'The Prince.' Mrs. Templeton squeezed between Gideon and Morcom, and she pointed with a slender, nicely shaped forefinger at the left hand. Gideon glanced at it and then at the portrait in the frame; there was no doubt at all about the difference in the thumbs. Mrs. Templeton was quite right.

"Thank you," Morcom said.

"No doubt about it." Gideon agreed. "I—" He broke off, seeing Thwaites, with an attendant, hovering in one of the two doorways. "Ah, Chief Inspector." Thwaites came forward;

Gideon made brief introductions; Thwaites called in more men. "The one *urgent* matter," Gideon said, "is whether to open the gallery to the public."

"I should, sir," Thwaites advised. "If we could have just this room - and perhaps those leading directly to it - closed for the time being, that should be enough for us. Too many people have walked about already for there to be any point in keeping the whole place shut."

"That's a relief!" said Morcom with obvious satisfaction. He turned to one of the senior attendants. "You'll do what's necessary, Smith, won't you? And I needn't ask you to give Chief Inspector Thwaites and his men every possible assistance, need I?"

"Be absolutely sure I will, sir," said Smith.

"And as soon as you can let Mrs. Templeton—" began Morcom.

"Oh, *please* don't rob me of my privileged position," the artist said. "If there could be a cup of coffee occasionally, I would be *enthralled* to stay here. And I know the gallery very well. I might even be useful."

There was a general laugh before Gideon and Morcom went off. They did not speak until they were at the main hall, when Morcom asked: "What about the press, Commander?"

"No need to keep anything from them unless you want to," Gideon answered. "My advice would be to tell them everything - you will probably need their help before long." As Morcom nodded, Gideon said, "I'll tell my men outside to regulate the flow of people coming in."

"You're very helpful," Morcom said. "Thank you for everything."

Gideon nodded, and went out.

The crowd outside was now at least a thousand strong - perhaps nearer two thousand - and a dozen policemen were controlling them, but the police had to stand in the road and there was a diversion barrier at the turning into the North Vestibule. A police sergeant pushed through the crowd and met

Gideon at the foot of the steps.

"Any news from inside, sir?"

"No," said Gideon. "They're going to open the doors in a few minutes. Let them in a couple of dozen at a time."

"I'll do that, sir."

"We're going in!" a girl cried out.

"They're opening the doors!" a man called.

Gideon, aware of a dozen cameras trained on him, saw a television team on the other side of the road, their backs to the fountains and Nelson's Column, the camera whirring. Reporters were also thick on the ground, and as they asked questions, he gave the same stock answer: "Chief Inspector Harold Thwaites is in charge. . . . He'll answer any questions that Mr. Morcom can't."

No one pressed for more.

Gideon reached the end of the street, where the road led round toward the steps of St. Martin's and Leicester Square. He crossed over, and stood on the top step. The crowd looked huge from here, the kind of scene that was commonplace at a political demonstration or a ban-the-bomb rally. Yet masses of people still stayed with the pigeons; probably half of them had no idea of what was happening at the National Gallery.

Well, they would know when the evening newspapers came out!

He walked to Whitehall, then along it toward Parliament Square, enjoying the feel of the pavement beneath his feet, glad he had sent the car back. There was something in the very air and look and feel of London that warmed and touched him with both affection and pride. He paused as he always did for a fraction of a minute opposite the Cenotaph, then went on. When he had first paid that respect to the dead, it had been out of a great sense of gratitude to those who had died. Now? Had it become virtually a habit? Was there in fact a little stubbornness in the pause, a conscious effort to make himself do what he felt he should?

He could not honestly be sure.

Once past the Cenotaph, he moved more briskly and, within five minutes, was in his office. There was a note on his desk: "Honiwell would like ten minutes - I've told him 2.30. I'm up in Records. A." Gideon sat down, pulled a telephone toward him and dialled the number of the Commander, Uniformed Branch, his opposite number.

There was no immediate answer, and for the first time that morning Gideon had a few moments to relax. In those moments, everything that had been discussed since he had reached the office passed through his mind in swift, fragmentary thoughts.

The Commander, Uniform, answered at last.

"Hallo, Charles," said Gideon. "Gideon here. You chaps are a bit pushed over at the National Gallery. Did you know about the theft?"

"Yes," the other replied. "I had an extra dozen men detailed."

"I should have known! With a bit of luck, the real pressure on them will be off in an hour, but there'll be more than the usual crowd all day and the press will be in strength, too."

"We'll cope," said Uniform dryly. "Any news yet?"

"Looks like a very clever job to me," Gideon said cautiously.

"These art thefts," remarked Uniform. "You can never be sure what they will do with what they take. Had much art-theft trouble lately?"

"No more than usual," Gideon answered. "Thanks, Charles." He rang off, knowing that if he hadn't made the call it might have looked as if he were usurping Uniform's authority. The different departments at the Yard worked together extremely well, but the machinery needed oiling sometimes. He was reminded of his rage when the Assistant Commissioner had tried to teach him his job. He laughed, but it didn't seem really funny.

His interoffice telephone rang, and he lifted the receiver.

"Gideon."

"Sorry to worry you," a man said, and immediately Gideon recognized the voice of Superintendent Thomas Riddell, who was in charge of the investigation into the smuggling of Pakistanis into the country. "Can you spare me half an hour or so?"

"When?" asked Gideon.

"Now, if possible," said Riddell. "I think you should know what I've discovered."

"All right, in fifteen minutes," Gideon said, and rang off.

Riddell had annoyed him, as Riddell often did. It was difficult to put a finger on the reason, except that the man too often presumed. It was more his manner than anything Gideon could really identify.

He rang for a messenger.

"Get me some coffee," he ordered. "Nothing to eat; I'm in a hurry." With anyone else, he might have said, "Bring a pot and two cups," but on this occasion it did not occur to him; he didn't want even a slightly social relationship with Riddell.

He did need to brief himself on the case Riddell was preparing.

9: Cause for Disquiet

There were problems in the life of a policeman which did not occur in the lives of others - not even in those of highly placed civil servants. No policeman, for instance, could outwardly espouse a political cause, because that would imply some degree of bias or prejudice. And no matter what he felt, no policeman could express his opinions of certain other aspects of the life of the community. Two problems arose out of this for Gideon. First, it cut a policeman off from communication with his fellow men, never a good thing; and second, it made difficulties in finding out the truth, since it was seldom possible, without this communication, to understand both sides of any question; one could listen but could not discuss wisely.

Yet a policeman had certain prejudices, certain interests, certain enthusiasms, and a policeman had instinctive reactions which training and self-discipline could never prohibit.

Above all, a policeman had to see a man *as* a man, not prejudge him because of colour or creed, or even because he had a record as long as his arm. Such absolute objectivity was never easy, and however liberal or understanding one was, even if one had not the slightest racialist feeling, it was impossible not to be aware of the tensions over colour in England. There were the Fascist types who hated black or coloured people without cause or reason, and there were more, so many more, who had come to believe that the immigrants did harm to the society, the community, even to the economy. Moreover, there were those who accepted the immigrants without question provided they were in the next town, or at least in a different section of their own town.

Policemen must not have prejudices, and yet prejudice existed, and the subject of racialism was as rife at the Yard as it would be anywhere else.

The messenger brought in a cup of steaming coffee, with plenty of cream and only a little sugar. Gideon had barely pushed the empty cup aside when there was a tap at the door.

"Come in," he called.

The first thing that struck him about Riddell was how the man had aged. He was handsome in his heavy-jowled way, though his brown hair was now streaked with silver, and his eyes, which had once been bright, were dull. He had put on weight, too.

"Good morning, Commander."

"Morning," Gideon grunted. "Come and sit down." Riddell sat and began to fumble in his pocket. "Smoke?" asked Gideon, pushing cigarettes across his desk.

"Ah, thanks," Riddell said. He took one and lit up. Even then, he seemed to have some difficulty in coming to what he had to say, and Gideon prompted him.

"What's this you've found out?"

"The smuggling is very widespread," Riddell announced positively. 'There's much more of it than I realized, or else I'm being pessimistic."

Gideon nodded, puzzled because the man was obviously troubled; he almost warmed to him.

"The fact is that at least three men are involved," stated Riddell, at last. "I can't offer proof yet, but it's only a matter of time before I'll be able to. Two of the men are Londoners, the third is an Indian - one of the early immigrants himself. None of them has ever been involved in crime before; certainly none has any record of any kind. The two Londoners own a lot of slum or near-slum property; the Indian rents the houses from them and lets off rooms at exorbitant rents. There's a day shift and a night shift for the beds, if you know what I mean.

Wouldn't wonder if they share the women, too, although God knows there are enough of them to go round."

He paused, and the way he looked at Gideon suggested that he knew that Gideon, in those last few seconds, had hardened against him.

Gideon waited, and after a moment's silence Riddell spoke again: "Oh, to hell with it, George! I can't stand them. I don't think they should ever have been allowed in. Give them a few years and they'll have flooded us out. If I had my way, I'd send them back bloody fast!" Riddell got up and began to walk about, speaking in a low-pitched voice and drawing fiercely at his cigarette. Gideon, startled by the outburst and concerned with Riddell's obvious emotion, did not interrupt. "That's how I *feel,"* went on Riddell. "I don't mind admitting that when you gave me this job I rubbed my hands. Now I can get some of the bastards, I told myself; now I can send them back where they belong." He spun round and faced Gideon, his eyes suddenly ablaze. "I saw one of the immigrants who'd been smuggled in three weeks ago. He lives in a hole under the stairs; there's no other word for it - rat-infested and filthy. It made me want to vomit when I saw it. And he's got no money, hardly any food. Lives more like an animal than a human being."

He moved stiffly toward the desk, stubbed out the cigarette, took another and lit it, and moved back two paces.

Gideon nodded, not 'wanting to interrupt in case he stopped the flow and so dried up the passion.

"These bloody sharks took all the money he had, promised him work he can't get, and will let him rot," Riddell said. "Now there are two damned good reasons for wanting to stop the smuggling."

Again, Gideon nodded.

"And where does that leave me?" demanded Riddell. "Right in the middle, George. I can't think straight about it. I can't even think for myself over it, let alone think as a copper. I'll tell you something else. Every time I look at one of them, I think Out, you bitch, or Out, you son-of-a-bitch, and if I had a man working for me who was half as full of hate, I'd fire him. That's what I really discovered, George. I can't go on with the job; it's got me facing two bloody ways. So—will you take me off?"

Gideon pursed his lips, then bent down, took out whisky and two glasses and a siphon of soda, and poured a stiff drink for Riddell and a mild one for himself.

"Cheers," he said. "I'd like to think about it, Tom."

"Do you really have to?" Riddell put the glass to his lips, muttered "Cheers," and drank deeply. He had needed that drink.

"Yes," Gideon said. "Yes, I do. How long have you been feeling like this?"

"About a week," answered Riddell gruffly. "Tell me I ought to have told you before and agree. George—*Commander*—rather than go on with this job, I'd resign. I'm not joking: I'd *resign*. I can go any time; a year or so won't make any difference."

"A few days won't make any difference, either," Gideon reasoned. He knew that in fact if Riddell resigned now instead of waiting until he was fifty-five, he would lose a substantial proportion of his pension. "I'll see you this time on Friday, with a decision."

"It won't make any diff—" began Riddell, and then broke off, and gave an almost sheepish grin "Sorry. Ought to know better than to think you couldn't think up something to make me change my mind. Thank—er—thanks for letting me blow my top." He finished his drink. "Twelve o'clock Friday, then."

"Yes." Gideon tapped the report. "Is this up to date?"

"On facts, yes."

"But not on your assessment of the facts?"

"I don't trust myself to make an assessment," Riddell muttered.

"Well, I do. And I want one by ten o'clock Friday morning," Gideon ordered. "Your handwriting will do, no need to get it typed. But I don't want anything left out, Tom; I want the lot."

After a pause, Riddell answered, in a much milder voice, "Yes, of course: I'll do it, make a thorough job of it. And the report may shock you, George."

"From what you say, there may be a lot to be passed on to the Home Office," said Gideon.

"I'm no bloody welfare officer," said Riddell. "But you're right." He paused again. "Anything else you want from me?"

"No, thanks."

"Right!" Riddell put his glass down, and went toward the door. "See you."

He went out.

Gideon felt as if he had lived through a sudden, furious storm and, when the door closed, was almost breathless. He sat, Buddha-like, for several minutes, and then suddenly he laughed; but there was no humour in the laugh and little in his expression. He had not expected to forget the Velazquez theft so quickly, but it had gone right out of his mind.

One of his telephones rang, startling him. He let it ring for a few minutes before lifting the receiver.

"Gideon here."

"Hallo, George. How are tricks?" It was the brisk and breezy voice of Lemaitre, whom Gideon had been thinking about earlier in the day. "Gotta bit of news for you I thought you'd like to know."

"What's that?" asked Gideon cautiously.

"I'm pretty sure I know where they're making the new decimal-coinage slush," stated Lemaitre.

"Pretty sure" was characteristic of him, and nine times out of ten he would be right. But on the tenth occasion he might simply have built up a case out of a single piece of information into which he had read a great deal of significance.

"Sounds good," Gideon said, still cautiously. "Where?"

"An old foundry, in my manor. A place on the river, George. Only about a mile from the Mint itself - how about that? What I want to do is raid the place."

"When?" asked Gideon.

"Tonight," answered Lemaitre. "Nothing like striking while the iron's hot, George - or catching the metal while it's molten."

Lemaitre could hardly control a guffaw of laughter, so pleased was he by that turn of phrase. "The thing is, I'd need some help from the Thames Division."

"Asked them yet?" inquired Gideon

"No," said Lemaitre. "Wanted to clear it with you first"

There was much more than there appeared to be behind that simple statement: a hint of some feeling or conflict between Lemaitre's division, on the land, and the Thames Division. It was a good thing to be warned such tension existed, just as it would be a bad thing to show that he felt it.

"How much help would you need?" asked Gideon, suddenly realizing that in fact Lemaitre might want much more than it was reasonable for one division to ask of another.

"Oh, a couple of patrol boats, in case we flush our birds and they try a getaway on the river," said Lemaitre, and added airily: "Nothing much, really."

Gideon grunted. "I'll have a word with Thames," he promised.

"Thanks a lot, Gee-Gee," Lemaitre said, with more heartfelt thanks than the situation merited.

Gideon rang off and immediately put a call through to Thames Division. The Superintendent in charge wasn't in, and he was put through at last to Chief Inspector Singleton, who had just completed a successful investigation into the use of the Thames for distributing stolen jewels.

"Good morning, sir," said Singleton.

"Nice job you've just tidied up," remarked Gideon.

"Good of you to say so," replied Singleton. "Easy enough when I knew the angle, though. What can I do for you, sir?"

"You can have a couple of launches standing by tonight to liaise with a land raid by NE Division." Gideon knew that he might get a reaction from Singleton which he would not get even from the Superintendent in charge.

To his astonishment, Singleton chuckled as if with high delight.

"So it worked," he said.

"What worked?"

"The tactics I used with old Lem!" There was a brief pause, and then, obviously as Singleton remembered he was speaking to the boss, a sharp exclamation and silence.

"All right, let's have it," growled Gideon.

"Er—sorry, sir," said Singleton. "It—er—it's nothing really. One or two of Mr. Lemaitre's men and one or two of ours have been getting on each other's nerves lately, and Mr. Lemaitre knows it, so instead of coming direct to me, he came to you. Bit silly, really, but you know what we old coppers are."

"I know," said Gideon. "Better make it three launches."

"Will Mr. Lemaitre get in touch with us about details?"

"Yes," Gideon said, any annoyance he had felt fading. "Bit silly" was right: policemen of such age and experience should not behave like children, but it happened sometimes and out in the divisions a sense of isolation could develop, breeding pettiness. In place of his annoyance was a question he wanted to ask, but he could not bring himself to do so. Last year, a Metropolitan Police officer named Carmichael with a long and distinctive record had attempted to murder his wife. The officer, a friend of Singleton's, had been tried and found guilty; he was serving a sentence of ten years' imprisonment. His wife was now living with another man, a most likable man, who would marry her the moment the divorce came through. There had been talk of Carmichael suing for divorce from prison, but Gideon had heard nothing about this for some time.

Singleton was the most likely person to have any news.

All these things flashed though Gideon's mind in a split second. Then Singleton said: "There's one other thing, sir, while you're on."

Carmichael?

"What?" asked Gideon.

"You remember the time Jenkins was mixed up in that art theft - the time we nobbled him when he was trying to get away in a cargo boat with some of the loot?"

Gideon's interest flared up.

"Yes, I remember very well."

"Funny thing about him killing himself or being accidentally gassed last night, wasn't it?" Singleton observed. "Especially as his old pal Slater was murdered in Brighton last night, too. One of our patrol-boat crews saw them together on the embankment the other day, and reported it when they heard what had happened. They had to go in close to have a look at some flotsam. *Very* peculiar, isn't it, sir?"

"Yes," Gideon said. He could pretend that he knew about Jenkins's death, or he could leave Singleton with a real glow by telling the truth. "I knew about Slater," he said. "Jenkins is news to me. Thanks." Then he added, with a faint laugh in his voice, "Look after N.E. Division, won't you?"

He rang off on Singleton's delighted chuckle, but did not echo that laughter as he pressed for Hobbs, knowing he might still be in Records.

But Hobbs came in, and they began to speak simultaneously.

"Have you heard—" Hobbs broke off.

"Have you heard—" Gideon broke off. "About Jenkins?" Hobbs asked quickly. "Just," said Gideon. "Why didn't I know before?"

10: Two in One

Lucy Jenkins heard the shop doorbell ring, and put down a rag with which she'd been dusting an old, very fragile Italian carved frame. She also heard footsteps above and they were reassuring. The Fisks were home, and she need make no decisions of her own, so it did not trouble her when she saw Red Thomas halfway between the door and the stack of pictures. He glanced at her almost furtively and said something she did not understand.

"Sorry about this, Lucy."

Mechanically, she said: "That's all right."

"Can I have another dekko?"

"Take as long as you like."

He began to go over the pictures again, and she noticed that instead of making a quick glance he was examining each one more closely, obviously hoping to find some special picture. One part of her mind, the part which trained itself, reflected that he must have sold the two pheasants well and the buyers had sent him back to see if there were others by the same artist. She was familiar with his peculiar form of nervous tension, the way he would stand back, rake a picture from every angle, and then turn it over and put it away with finicky precision.

Then she saw two men on the other side of the road, looking toward the shop. One was a policeman and - again with the self-trained part of her mind - she knew that the second one was a plainclothes detective. She was not alarmed in any way but a little sorry for Red, because obviously the police were investigating him.

"Red," she said, in a quiet voice.

"Hey?" He didn't look up.

"There are two policemen watching you."

"So let them watch."

If *he* wasn't concerned, there was no reason why she should be, so she went on with cleaning the picture. Something fell heavily upstairs: Old Fisky, dropping a boot; it was always such a performance when he put his big heavy boots on. The two policemen came across the road, and Lucy ducked out of sight but listened. She had a strange sense of panic, a carry-over from those early days when the police had come for her father, as they so often had.

The doorbell clanged.

The sounds above were heavier but not so loud - Old Fisky, walking about to get his feet comfortable in his boots. Lucy had subdued but frightening palpitations and leaned against the bench, rag in her right hand, left hand supporting her body against the wall.

A man said, "Is Miss Jenkins in?"

She could hardly believe she had heard right. These men wanted *her*.

Red said, swallowing the words, "In the back."

A man called out, "Miss Jenkins, are you there?"

They had come for *her*.

Her panic rose wildly; her heart thumped like the clumping of Old Fisky's boots. They had come for her, and she hadn't done a thing. She just worked here, just did what she was told. She felt so weak that the frame slipped and a piece of the gilt carving broke off. She could hear her own breathing, as if she were drawing and exhaling breath through some kind of fog.

"Miss Jenkins?"

The two men appeared in the doorway, the uniformed one in front. She saw him but did not understand the expression on his face. He was young and not very big or impressive He had a broad nose, rather squashed, and a slight hare lip, not enough to deform or to give him any speech impediment; and he had big features and the softest, brownest eyes. But all she saw was a face beneath a policeman's helmet. She almost fainted, was aware of the man moving, and then, suddenly, that he was supporting her.

"Take it easy," he said very gently. "Take it easy."

A strange thing happened to Lucy Jenkins, something she did not understand, did not think about for some time. She felt calmed. The panic subsided and her breathing became much more even. The policeman had one arm round her shoulders and that arm seemed to blanket her with warmth.

He repeated, "Take it easy," and after a few moments asked, "Are you all right?"

"Yes—yes," she said huskily.

"You know, then," he said, still holding her.

"Know—know what?" she asked.

He did not respond immediately, and very slowly, almost with reluctance, he took his arm away. The plainclothesman was standing in the doorway leading to the shop, and Old Fisky was in the doorway leading from the stairs to the flat above - Old Fisky, a shrunken giant, clothes loose and baggy, his scraggy neck encircled by his big, deep collar. The policeman was now a yard away from her, oblivious of the others, and she became aware of his glowing brown eyes. She sensed something else, too, something remarkably like the protective warmth of his arm; soothing.

"I seem to have jumped to conclusions," he said. "Obviously you don't know."

Both the other men had the sense to stand still and silent.

Lucy made an effort, and asked, "What am I supposed to know?"

"About your father," the policeman answered.

She was startled into harshness, spurred by a bitterness which was part of her.

"Oh, *him*. Has he been picked up again?"

"No," the policeman said gently, and he drew a step further

away. "He died yesterday."

The word "died" made no immediate impression on her at first, and rather stupidly she echoed without thinking, "Died?"

"I'm sorry. Yes."

She began to realize what she was being told and, in a different kind of panic, cried:

"But—but I didn't know he'd been ill!"

"He hadn't been ill," the man said.

"You mean he had an *accident?*" Real concern showed for the first time, and she felt an easing of the harshness and the bitterness she had always felt toward her father.

"A kind of accident," he told her. "He was gassed in his room. The gas was turned on, and he dropped off to sleep."

Lucy suddenly remembered that her father had always been very careful with gas. This was the last thing she would have expected. But she did not say so. "Never speak without thinking and never talk to the cops," her father's voice seemed to say in her mind at that moment.

"Poor old sod," she said flatly.

"You had no idea?" asked the policeman.

"Not the faintest."

"When did you last see him?" the plainclothesman asked. He had a grating voice and a hard face and cold, cold eyes. As he spoke, Old Fisky moved for the first time, not interrupting and not distracting the others. He reached the desk behind Lucy and stood still, looking down at the gilded frame and the small chip that had fallen off it.

Lucy seemed to consider for a long time, and then she said, "It would be three years ago last Christmas."

"What?" exclaimed the plainclothesman.

"Good God!" said the policeman. "You haven't seen him for nearly *four years?*"

"No," answered Lucy, and after a long silence she went on: "And I didn't want to. He didn't want to see me, either."

"Did you write to him or communicate in any way?" asked the plainclothesman.

"No, we didn't have anything to do with each other after he came out of prison," she answered. "We didn't have anything in common - we never did, really."

"There's one thing you did do," said Old Fisky, startling them by speaking; he had a very deep, unexpectedly firm voice. "You sent him a Christmas card with a five-pound note in it, every year."

"Supposing I did?" Lucy coloured deeply as if caught out in some shameful deed. "After all, he was my father." She looked defiantly from the policemen to Old Fisky. "It's none of your business, anyway."

"I know, my dear," the old man croaked. "I shouldn't have spoken out of turn."

"Forget it," said Lucy, straightening up.

The plainclothesman switched to Fisk: had he seen Lucy's father, or the man Slater, Dicey Slater? No. Had they been in the shop - sometimes they acted as runners for collectors and buyers. No. Had anyone been in here lately, for any special artist? No. Had he heard of any buyer, underground, who would buy valuable paintings without asking questions? No. Had he had any strangers in? Strangers were always coming in. Had he had any strangers in, buying for the trade? He wouldn't know about that if they didn't tell him. If he heard of any big undercover buyers, would he be sure to tell the police? Yes, of course, he always cooperated with the police.

"I'll look in once or twice a day," the policeman said, with an air of great righteousness.

The plainclothesman nodded, and the two policemen went out, glancing at but not talking to Red Thomas; obviously the plainclothesman had wanted him to hear. When they had gone, Old Fisky put a hand quite impersonally on Lucy's shoulder, but didn't speak. Red appeared in the doorway, eyes darting from one to the other.

"What's up, Mr. Fisk?" he asked.

"How should I know," Fisk replied. "Is there anything you want?"

Red hesitated, then said, "I bought those two pheasants by an unknown. Got any more by the same kind of artist? I'm only asking, see."

"Pheasants? No, but I'll keep my eyes open," Fisk promised. "I've bought quite a lot of pictures from an old house in Somerset. They'll be ready tomorrow, and I'll have a look." He nodded, and Red went out, backing, turning, half running.

"That man always makes me think he started late and is trying to catch up," remarked Fisk. "Want to talk about your Pa?" When she shook her head, he went on: "Your note said there was something you wanted me to have a look at. Which one is it?"

"It's this." Lucy bent down and took the picture from beneath the bench. "It's an old canvas that was painted over. I took off the muck and began to clean it at the corner and it looked different to me, so I had a closer look and it's an old canvas stuck on a newer one, so I tried to separate them and I thought I might do some damage and I stopped. Was that right?"

Fisk was examining the picture, the cleaned corner, the new canvas. He turned it over and over in his hands. It seemed an age before he answered: "Well, Lucy, you were right!"

"Is it a find?" she wanted to know eagerly.

"We'll have a look at it this afternoon, and then I might be able to tell you," he promised. "But first I've got the van full of pictures from Somerset. I'd like to get them in here before lunchtime, as I may need the van again."

"Give me the key," volunteered Lucy, "and I'll unload."

Old Fisky took the van keys out of his pocket and handed them to her. When she had gone, he took a watchmaker's glass from the pocket of his thick tweed waistcoat and examined the cleaned corner very closely. He sniffed, wrinkling his nose, nodded, and put the glass away.

Lucy came in with several heavy pictures hugged close to her bosom, as if she were holding a lover.

At a little after one o'clock that day, Christine Falconer parked her red mini near Lancelot Judd's shop in Hampstead, got out, long legs drawing glances from several young men passing by, and went along to the shop. Lance was inside, talking to Robin Kell, a tall youth wearing a green velvet jacket, peach-coloured close-fitting pants, and suede shoes. He was a better-looking man than Lance, but not so tall and not so powerful in build. His hair, cut long but not overlong, curled almost like a girl's.

Lance's eyes brightened at sight of Christine.

"Hallo, darling! On time as usual."

"The irreproachable Christine," observed the other. "Good morning, *darling.*"

"Hallo, Robin," she said carelessly. "I hate being late."

"*Or* being kept waiting," remarked Robin. "The privileges of being born with a diamond-encrusted spoon in your pretty mouth."

"What a dear, sweet person you are," retorted Christine. "Why *you* were ever born at all I can't imagine. Lance, I do want to talk to you. *Alone,* please."

"I can take even the subtlest of hints," said Robin. "If I may just wait for my beloved, who is spending a penny. Ah!" He paused, as water flushed and a W.C. clanked. "She is about to join us." A moment later, a girl appeared, tall, beautifully made-up, and rather exotic-looking. "Hurry up, *cherie,*" he urged. "Christine has some perfectly breathtaking news for Lance which she doesn't want us to share."

"She knows she couldn't trust you with a secret for five minutes," the girl said. "And just in case she didn't realize that instinctively, I warned her." She took Robin by the hand and led him out, saying, "Bye, Chris. Bye, Lance."

"See you soon," Christine called.

"Bye, Robin—bye, Marie." Lance Judd waved as the others went out, then turned to Christine, now at the back of the shop, which was long and narrow, with an alcove leading off: a hand basin, a kettle, and a few oddments of pottery on one side, the narrow door to the W.C. on the other. The "kitchen" was remarkably like the corner of Leslie Jenkins's room, but every cup, mug, bowl, and saucer was artistic.

Christine was no longer smiling, and in repose looked remarkably like her father, with his high bridged nose and arched lips.

"Why so serious, sweetheart?" Lance asked her, lightly but not flippantly, and when she didn't answer at once, he went on: "You like Robin less and less, don't you?"

"Yes," Christine answered slowly. "I know he's an old friend of yours and I wish I didn't dislike him, but—" She broke off, took Lance's hands, and said with obvious depth of feeling, "Be careful, Lance. Don't let him use you."

"Oh, I know Robin and his tricks," said Lance, still lightly. "I also know that he insults you to try to persuade you that he isn't interested in your father's wealth and doesn't see him as a big buyer. But he does, you know. He doesn't fool *me*."

She looked at him almost suspiciously, and said: "I hope he doesn't. I really hope he doesn't." Then she seemed to push her anxiety away, and changed the subject. "Lance, Daddy *is* having me watched. I can't do anything about it. I wish—"

She broke off as the door opened and a policeman in uniform and a man in plainclothes came in.

11: The Questioners

All over London, police visits were being made and police questions were being asked, questions like those asked of Old Fisky. Every antique dealer, every dealer in pictures and prints, in *objets d'art* and in old jewellery, was being checked and checked again. The range of inquiry was almost unbelievable. There were the dealers in London's Mayfair, in Knightsbridge and the City, dealers who bought and sold paintings worth thousands or tens of thousands as if they were oddments off a market stall. There were the great auction rooms of Sotheby's and Christie's, and the smaller rooms where only dealers with a discerning eye were likely to make bids.

There were the antique "supermarkets" in different parts of London, Chelsea and the West End, bigger than the others, markets where everything might be found, from precious porcelain to old silver, from Roman coins to Japanese samurai swords. There were necklaces and Spanish combs, bric-a-brac from all corners of the earth, brought to England by traveller, adventurer, tradesman, or soldier, once to grace a home, now resting, as it were, between one home and the next.

In the galleries and the great salesrooms, the finest art ever known to man was bought and sold at prices so far beyond the reach of ordinary people that they watched and heard and marvelled. How could - why should - a piece of canvas used for a painting five, four, three, two centuries, even a single century ago command such value? And how could some men, individuals like other human beings, acquire or inherit such wealth that they could afford to pay such prices?

But although many millions of people were not directly affected, there being a wide gap between them and such a concept of the value of art, wherever pictures were purchased for the nation this gap narrowed. It made way for a kind of closeness, since art that belonged to the nation belonged in fact to all. The public might not comprehend the technical skill of these works - might not always fully appreciate their beauty - but nevertheless there was an understanding of the value of masterpieces and a certain pride in their shared possession.

There was, furthermore, an understanding of the lust some men felt for the great paintings, an understanding of the near mania that some felt in their passion to possess. And, fed skilfully by the newspapers, there was understanding also of the men who stole and sold, the leaders of the gangs who had the illegal market under their control. And every now and again some such theft caught the public imagination until a whole nation was agog at the daring of the men who stole; and in this was a touch of admiration, often very strong if no one had been hurt in the theft.

The theft of "The Prince" from the National Gallery had caught the public's imagination, for no one, not even the newspapermen, had yet realized that two men had been murdered after their part in the theft. The cleverness of the raid, the skill and precision with which it had been done, won not only admiration from the man in the street but a grudging kind of praise in some of the national newspapers. And it was against this background that the police in London carried out their visitations. No second hand shop - even one masquerading as "antiques" - no gallery, no saleroom, no warehouse was missed. Each visit was made by a uniformed man working with a plainclothesman, giving the proper touch of authority, and after each visit a detailed report was put into division and a copy sent to New Scotland Yard.

And the Yard geared itself for one of the biggest searches in London's history, under Commander George Gideon.

On Friday, the third day after the discovery of the theft, public interest began to wane, headlines became smaller, and the story vanished from the front pages and became easily lost inside the papers. There were several semi-sarcastic leading articles, directed largely at the weakness of security precautions at the galleries and the inadequacy of the police. One newspaper put it scathingly:

> The consistent failure, not only of the Metropolitan Police in London, but of the provincial police forces, to recover valuable works of art, whether stolen from publicly or privately owned galleries and homes, is a matter of grave concern. How is it possible for thieves to plot, prepare, and carry out such triumphant raids as the recent theft of "*The Prince*" - almost as famous now as the once stolen Goya?
> When the Goya was stolen, one man, unaided, apparently outwitted both galleries and the police. Now more than one are doing the same, and the police appear to be helpless - or inadequate.
> What is the reason?
> One must face the possibility that the police, no matter how good they may be in most phases of their activity, are not interested when the nation's cultural properties are at stake. If there is the slightest truth in this, then a completely new approach is not only necessary, it is essential.

After reading this, Gideon sat back in his chair and pursed his lips, staring forbiddingly at the window that overlooked the Thames. It was some time before he pulled his reports toward him; there were other problems to be considered, too. He came back to Riddell's report and its assessment of the immigration smuggling, but three times in succession he was stopped on its first page by the telephone, none of the calls important. He was halfway through the report, and had not yet reached Riddell's assessment, when his door opened abruptly, without the usual warning tap, and Wilson Chamberlain, the Assistant Commissioner, came in. A recently retired Member of Parliament and one-time regular army officer, he was a handsome man who held himself very erect and spoke with a slightly shrill tone which often made him sound querulous. Gideon, acutely aware of his personal dislike of the man, felt himself stiffen, but even as he did so he warned himself not to allow prejudice to blind him to the other's qualities.

"Ah, Gideon." Chamberlain closed the door behind him and advanced toward the desk. "We need a survey of the investigation into the National Gallery robbery as quickly as possible."

"Why?" asked Gideon flatly, and realized at once that he had also got off on the wrong foot. "I mean—is there any particular reason?"

"Certainly. There is to be a conference Monday morning," Chamberlain said.

Gideon just stopped himself from asking, "A conference of whom?" and said, "The survey is always up-to-date, sir, but so far not particularly helpful."

"'We need details of what has been done, what leads we have - everything."

"For whom, sir?"

"Does that matter?"

"It can matter very much," Gideon told him. "If it's for Yard use, then a lot can be taken for granted; they know the background. If it's for Home Office or other officials, then a great deal more explanatory detail is required. Some details can be filled in at a meeting, but everyone who attends needs a grounding. A briefing can be prepared in an hour and copies can be available an hour after that."

"Good," Chamberlain said. "Good. The Home Office has been pressing the Commissioner for the survey, and the Ministry of Public Works and Buildings wants to be represented as well, of course, as the Arts Council and, naturally, the keepers and custodians of the various galleries. We will, of course, wish to be well represented ourselves."

Chamberlain stopped speaking and drew back, and Gideon had a feeling that he was asking for approval. "See how much I know of how these things should be done," Chamberlain was implying. Gideon, aware of this and of his own feeling of resentment, also became aware of the funny side of it: and it *was* funny! What had happened to the Home Secretary to appoint such a man? Gideon's thoughts veered back. How could he live with such a situation and contrive to use this man to the department's advantage? After all, he *had* to live with him.

"Very comprehensive," he said, at last. "What time is this—ah—conference to be called, sir?"

"Is ten o'clock reasonable?"

"I think eleven would enable us to get everything ship-shape," Gideon replied. "Will the Commissioner be present?"

"I trust so. I *expect* so. He is at the Scarborough Conference today."

"Ah, yes," said Gideon, who hadn't known that the Commissioner of the Metropolitan Police was away and who now understood that Chamberlain had been making hay while the sun shone. "Where do you propose to have the conference?"

"Where would you suggest, Commander?"

"In the main Conference Room. There will be twenty at least, I imagine."

"Yes, indeed, and possibly more. And can you have the preliminary surveys available for distribution this afternoon?"

"You make out the list, sir, and we'll get them delivered," Gideon promised.

"Excellent. That's excellent." Chamberlain nodded, made a right about turn, and stepped with military precision to the door. "I would like two copies," he announced, and went out.

Very slowly, but in a much better mood, Gideon shook his head. Soon he reread the editorial, wondered what Chamberlain would have said had he read it, then reluctantly put Riddell's report aside and studied the bigger report on the art theft. Hobbs had prepared this during the night, and Gideon realized now how carefully it had been done; it was almost as if Hobbs had anticipated what would be needed. After making a few additions and deletions, he rang for Hobbs, who came in at once.

"I hear you've had a visitor," he remarked.

"I gather you anticipated it," said Gideon. "Is there anything more in?"

"No," said Hobbs "We've had a hundred and twelve more negative reports, and we estimate that by now over sixty percent of the dealers in the London area have been questioned." He stood just where Chamberlain had, and Gideon could remember feeling hostile toward *him* on occasions over the years, but never as hostile as he felt toward the A.C.

What a pity Hobbs wasn't in Chamberlain's place; he would make a ten times better Assistant Commissioner!

The fleeting thought passed, and Gideon said, "You know what we ought to do next, don't you?"

"Go into the home counties and the provinces," said Hobbs.

"Yes. Get teletype requests out for them to do the same thing," ordered Gideon. "If I've jumped the gun, at least no one can cancel the instruction. Before you go, Alec—"

"Yes?"

"Anything at all about Jenkins and Slater?"

"Not that matters," answered Hobbs. "One lead to Jenkins might have been his daughter Lucy, but it proves that they've been estranged for years. That's a dead end And no useful fingerprints were on the gas meter at Jenkins's house."

"Not even Jenkins's own?"

"Faint and very smeared," Hobbs answered. "The report's in there." Gideon nodded, and Hobbs continued, "But there are a couple of things, no more than rumours, which Frobisher picked up. First, that Sir Richard Falconer isn't too particular where he buys, and second, that he has a secret strong room where he keeps pieces he has purchased knowing them to be stolen."

Aware that Hobbs was an acquaintance of Falconer's, Gideon said, "The same rumour touches most of the big collectors, you know."

"Yes, I know." Hobbs smiled. "Thanks!"

"Any reason at all to suspect Falconer?" asked Gideon.

"No," answered Hobbs. "And yet I've often realized that he's extremely careful about who sees his collection. His daughter certainly has some odd acquaintances, though. She was in an antique shop in Hampstead yesterday, a place owned by Lancelot Judd."

"Should I know much about him?" asked Gideon.

"Very prominent in C.N.D.," Hobbs reminded him.

"Oh, Lord, yes," said Gideon. "I remember." There had been a conflict between the police and youthful campaigners for nuclear disarmament a few years before, and a Lancelot Judd had been one of the leaders of demonstrations which had been very nearly riots in Trafalgar Square and Whitehall. But Judd had been quiet for a long time since then.

"Was Falconer's daughter ever involved in C.N.D.?" he asked.

"Not as far as we can find out," Hobbs answered. "But she and Judd are being watched in view of recent events, and we have discovered one interesting thing; her father's having her watched, too! Oliphant, personal assistant, is using a private inquiry agent."

Gideon raised an eyebrow. "Hmm. That's rather odd. And how's Thwaites doing at the gallery?"

"I gather he's done practically all he can there," answered Hobbs.

"Well, have him concentrate on this Falconer-Judd angle," Gideon ordered. "I'll talk to him and Frobisher this afternoon and see how they're getting on together. Meanwhile," he added with heavy humour, "I think you're going to be detailed to a conference at eleven o'clock on Monday morning." He explained to Hobbs, who simply shrugged, and then went on: "Riddell's due in soon. Have you given any thought to him and the immigration smuggling?"

"I read his report before you came in," said Hobbs. "He's obviously delved deeply, as he's got at a lot of the facts. But I get a strong impression there's a mental block in his approach. He's not as lucid and objective as he could and should be."

"What would you do? Keep him on or give the job to Honiwell?" asked Gideon.

"George," said Hobbs very slowly, "I wouldn't like to make the decision. I really wouldn't. But on balance I think I'd make him stay."

"Why?" asked Gideon.

"Because I think he'll find it difficult to live with himself if he's taken off," Hobbs said. "And he's so alive to the danger that I don't think he'll do anything out of prejudice now."

There was a tap at the passage door, and Gideon felt instinctively that it was Riddell. He called "Come in" and Riddell appeared, a grim-faced, hard-eyed Riddell, who looked as if he were prepared for a fight.

12: Tensions

One fact was immediately obvious; this was no time for Gideon to tell Riddell that he hadn't yet studied the report and not even reached the assessment. Clearly something had happened to affect the man like this, and to bring him to Gideon's office at least ten minutes early.

"I'll talk to Thwaites," Hobbs said, moving toward the door, and nodding to Riddell; but it was doubtful whether Riddell noticed or heard him. The communicating door closed quietly.

"Sit down," Gideon said to Riddell.

"I'd rather stand, I—"

"Sit *down,* I said!"

Now, suddenly, there was conflict between them, deliberately forced by Gideon. In this office particularly, and on the job in general, it would be disastrous to allow any subordinate to gain the upper hand, and Riddell was dangerously near making his own terms.

Slowly, Riddell sat down, but he perched on the edge of the armchair.

"What's brought you early?" asked Gideon.

"Early? I'm not—" Riddell glanced at his watch, then raised his hands and dropped them heavily onto his knees. "Sorry," he said. "But this job is pushing me hard."

"I can imagine," Gideon conceded. "It's a bad time all round. The National Gallery affair is causing a lot of trouble."

"Oh, that." Riddell gave the impression that he had hardly

heard of the theft and wasn't interested, anyway. Most men at the Yard were aware of the dangers in the situation, alive to the fact that if they failed to find "The Prince" soon the Yard's stock would fall heavily. But as these thoughts passed through Gideon's mind, Riddell sat back, pushed his fingers through his hair, and gave a snort of a laugh. "I see what you mean - my problem is one of many and you can't be as obsessed with it as I am. Good thing, too." He paused and Gideon waited. "You remember me telling you about a poor devil of an immigrant who was stowed away in a hole under some stairs?"

"Yes," said Gideon. "Vividly."

"I lied to you," said Riddell, and his eyes burned.

"Did you?" asked Gideon. He tried to sound casual and as if this really wasn't worth making a fuss about, but he was disturbed not only by the admission but also by Riddell's state of mind. "Why?"

"It wasn't a man; it was a girl."

Gideon said, almost blankly: "Oh."

"That's about the right reaction *'Oh,'* with your heart falling into your boots," said Riddell bitterly. "Yes, a girl. She was only a kid." *Was,* thought Gideon "Even though she was thin as a lath, all skin and bone, she was beautiful. Never seen such eyes. They did something to me, George. Imagine that! A hard-bitten, anti-black copper took one look into a pair of brown eyes and—Oh, I needn't spell it out. It made me seethe. She was a Pakistani, very dark-skinned, and she represented everything I didn't believe in. She belonged back home in Karachi or Lahore or wherever she came from; she should never have been brought here. I still think that," he went on fiercely. "But she got under my skin. She made me see what happens to a lot of them when they're over here. She was nothing but a frightened kid, and she didn't really have a chance."

Again Riddell paused.

"Go on, Tom," Gideon said gently.

"Well, I got the welfare people on to her, had her taken to hospital. She died early this morning. I telephoned the hospital and was told about it. No one's claimed her body. She was living in that rat hole, and the people who live in the house - I've found sixteen, so far - say they didn't know her. *She* told me that she'd been smuggled in and was told to hide in that cupboard until someone brought her some documents. She stayed there, and hardly ever went out. The others gave her scraps for food. She was there for nearly two months, but the documents never came."

Riddell pressed both hands against his forehead and brushed them over his greying hair. Gideon, watching, felt a kind of distress and anxiety and alarm, for if such a thing as this were repeated often, it would be - it was - not only a scandal but a crime against humanity. He had another feeling, too, of disquiet, because he did not know whether any of this was in Riddell's written assessment of the case. He guessed that it wasn't, because it burst out of the man as if it were something he had been holding back for a long time but which had become too much.

"How many instances are there like this?" asked Gideon.

"A bloody sight too many, *that's* for sure."

"Do you know who smuggled this girl in?" Gideon asked, then went on quickly, "I didn't know women were smuggled; I thought they were all men."

"Most of them are," answered Riddell. "Only girl I've heard of, in fact. The men come in, and after a while they get work and permits and then they begin to send for their relatives, wives by the dozen, they—"

"All right," Gideon interrupted. "I know how you feel now. You still need a lot more evidence before making a charge, don't you?"

"Yes."

"Do you still feel certain you want to be taken off the case?"

"I don't know what I feel," Riddell acknowledged, "except— well, I'd like to see the business cleared up once and for all."

"What about leave?" asked Gideon. "How much have you due?"

"Three weeks."

"Then take it," said Gideon, "and I'll assign Honiwell in charge while you're away, on a temporary basis. When you've had a break, we can take another hard look at the situation. If you want to get back into it, you can."

After a long pause, Riddell leaned back more relaxed then he had yet been, and said warmly: "The judgment of Gideon! It's a good idea. Thanks, George." After another pause, he went on, "If ever the right man was in the right job, you are." He stood up, hesitated, and then asked: "When would you like me to go?"

"Any time. This" - Gideon tapped the report - "is more than a start for Honiwell or anyone who stands in for you. Any reason why you shouldn't begin your holiday right away?"

"No," answered Riddell. "My wife will jump for joy."

"Right!" said Gideon. "I'll send a chit through." He stood up, big and towering, and put out his hand. "Have as good a time as you can."

Riddell shook hands, nodded, and went out; the door closed very firmly. Gideon moved across to the window and looked over a now sunlit river and London at its loveliest. He stood very still for a long time, not absolutely sure that he had done the right thing, but greatly moved by Riddell's story.

How easy it was to misjudge a man; how easy for a man to misjudge himself.

He hardly knew how long he had been standing there when his telephone buzzed, and he was glad to have to move.

"Gideon," he announced.

"Alec here," Hobbs said. "Are you free for a few minutes?"

"Yes. Come in."

"Right away," Hobbs said. His voice seemed hardly to have died away when the communicating door opened and he appeared. He had a sheaf of papers with him and Gideon saw the name "ENTWHISTLE" on the outside of a folder. Hobbs sat down, still holding the papers.

"How did it go with Riddell?" he asked, and Gideon told

him.

Hobbs smiled.

"The judgment of Solomon," he observed, and then went on without a change of tone: "Honiwell seems to have done all he can so far on the Entwhistle case, and it will probably have to sweat for a few weeks. He could fit as *locum* for Riddell very well." When Gideon simply nodded, he said, "Thwaites has finished at the National Gallery but he would like two of our men to stay there on the Security Force, and Morcom's quite agreeable."

"So am I," said Gideon.

"Thanks." Hobbs paused for a moment and then asked in a harder voice, "Have you time to talk about Entwhistle?"

"Yes," said Gideon, and he thought - as he often did - of the man in Dartmoor who might be innocent of the crime for which he had been sentenced to life imprisonment.

Entwhistle was out on the moor, breaking rocks.

When he had been leading his ordinary life, he had not seriously believed that prisoners still broke rocks with sledge hammers, but he had discovered that they did. The rocks could be used for road building and wall building; there was a kind of rhythm to the actual work and once one was used to it, it was no great strain. Entwhistle, tall and gaunt, had always been a strong man.

Now, lifting the long-handled sledgehammer ready for the downward swing, he saw the great expanse of the moor on this lovely autumn day, and the never-ending rocks themselves, more rocks than ten thousand convicts could break in a hundred years. He saw the rugged beauty and the green of distant trees and grass, the other men working, some naked to the waist, browned skin exposed to the sun and glistening from sweat. It was like a symphony of movement and a symphony of harsh and cacophonous sound. Chips of granite flew, big rocks split; now and again a man swore with desultory indifference or in sharp pain where a rock had cut him. Entwhistle, used to the heat of the tropics, an engineer who had helped build huge bridges across untamed rivers and great valleys, felt an awful sense of helplessness, of frustration. It was madness that he should be doing this, and it was driving him mad.

This was one of his bad days.

It was a day when he could not get his children out of his mind - the children he had not seen since he had been imprisoned, over three years before.

Three years for a crime he had not committed.

Three years in Dartmoor - for quarrelling with his wife, going home, and finding her dead.

Three years, while her killer was free, living life to the full, not conscience-stricken or he would have confessed or at least made some attempt to help him, Geoffrey Entwhistle.

Three years.

One for Carol, who was now seven, fair, and pretty.

One for Clive, who was now fourteen, tall, and eager.

One for Jennifer, who was now eleven and, so they told him, clever.

He could picture them not as they were but as they had been, so young and vital and overjoyed to see him on his return home, because he had been away for so much of their lives.

He could see their faces in the rocks.

Sometimes, when he brought that sledgehammer crashing down, it was as if he were crushing one of his beloved children; and in an awful way, by his very existence in this place, he was in fact crushing them. Prison, the law, the policeman who had sent him here, the judge and every bloody juror, the man who had actually killed his wife - each one had been a blow against his children's happiness; his children condemned to live under the brand of Cain, staying with relations, snubbed and sneered at and derided because of a crime their father had not committed.

Now and again, he glimpsed a kind of hope.

A prison-visiting parson named Wilkinson had once brought him much hope, saying that the police, through Commander

George Gideon, had promised to review the evidence, but that was nearly a year ago, and since then he had heard nothing at all but platitudes. Eventually Wilkinson had been appointed to a living overseas, and now it seemed that he had turned his back on this heart-breaking problem: and that no one cared.

Today, Entwhistle was vividly aware of each child, each hammer blow now seeming to crack and split their future, each blow robbing him of a little more hope, and each driving him a little more mad.

He *would* go mad if he didn't get out of this soul-destroying place.

He must escape.

Not tonight, but one day soon.

Better to be on the run, better to be shot while running, than to exist like this.

Better to be dead.

The thought came to him, not for the first time, that death would be the answer, putting an end not only to his own daily despair but to that of his children. No longer would they be burdened by the knowledge that he was in prison paying for the crime they believed he had committed, making some kind of amends for murdering their mother.

Oh, God, he could not stand it!

He whirled the hammer round and round as if it were a weight in an athlete's hand, went round and round with it, felt his head swimming, felt dizzy, felt as if he were going mad, mad, mad!

He let the hammer go.

It crashed thirty yards away and smacked against a boulder, letting out a dull metallic ring. He stood, swaying, staring. He was aware of a guard approaching, rifle cocked. His blood thundered through his ears and the refrain would not stop. He was going mad, mad,.

mad . . . .

"Did it slip?" asked the warder.

Slip?

"Eh?"

"Did it slip?" the warder asked again. *Slip?*

"It—yes. Yes, it slipped."

"Well, go and get it and be more careful," the warder ordered.

In his report to the Governor, the warder told a different story.

"I advise keeping Entwhistle within the precincts for some time, sir. He undoubtedly hurled his hammer, and nearly lost his self-control. I gave him to understand that I thought the hammer slipped - thought it might calm him down a bit."

"We'll have him back in the library," the Governor said.

In his tiny office which overlooked the Thames and a corner of Billingsgate Market, Eric Greenwood, the man who had been the lover of Geoffrey Entwhistle's wife, and who had killed her, was looking through samples of carpets shipped from India, from Pakistan, from Persia, and from Morocco. They were all beautifully hand-woven with a rich variety of colours particularly attractive in the afternoon light.

He was deciding whether to order or whether to wait for a week or two when the shipper's prices might come down.

He did not give a moment's thought to the past and to what he had done, and he felt absolutely secure in his sheltered bachelor life.

Gideon, sitting in his office, listened to Hobbs and, after ten minutes, sent for Chief Superintendent Honiwell, the man who was checking the evidence against Geoffrey Entwhistle. Gideon knew, as Honiwell did, that the threads were tenuous and the case tortuous, and before it could possibly be reopened, proof must be found that there had been a miscarriage of justice. Nothing less could justify a full reopening of the case.

Honiwell was a mild man, quiet-voiced, thorough, and painstaking, and above all humane.

Gideon contrasted the calmness of his demeanour with the

tensions there were in Riddell. Honiwell gave the impression that nothing could ever shake his composure or make him speak quickly or out of turn. He came in quietly, took the chair Gideon indicated, settled comfortably, and waited.

"So you think you've found the man we're looking for," Gideon said.

"I think so, sir. Once we established the fact that Mrs. Entwhistle *had* a lover, it was simply a question of time. If I'm right, sir, he's a man named Greenwood, works at a firm of importers and exporters who handle mostly Oriental goods - carpets, cloth, carvings, spices, a fairly general range. It's been a long job to locate him, as we didn't want the press to get wind of it, but he's been identified by at least seven people, mostly waiters, as having been with Mrs. Entwhistle a great deal while Entwhistle was abroad. We could make a good circumstantial case against him, but I don't think the time's ripe for that yet."

One thing was certain, Gideon thought when the others had left, Honiwell could not be taken off this case. Someone who was less involved in a case would have to take over from Riddell. He must talk to Hobbs again. Meanwhile, he needed to look through the Entwhistle file. Soon he found himself wondering bleakly what a man would feel like if he were in prison for a crime he had not committed. The more he pondered, the more urgent the case became.

His interoffice telephone rang, and he lifted it. It was Chamberlain.

"Ah, Gideon. Several of those who should be present can't make it on Monday, so make a change in your diary, will you? Same place; same time, Tuesday."

"Very good, sir," Gideon said. Then he replaced the receiver and said through his teeth. "We'll have that damned Velazquez back before the conference if I have to find it myself!"

A few seconds later, two senior Yard men, passing the door, heard Gideon burst out into a deep, hearty laugh. One of them remarked, "He's pleased with life, that's something."

"Perhaps they've found the Velazquez," the other said.

Hobbs, alone in the next office, lifted his head and listened, half expecting the door to open and Gideon to share the joke. But he realized, knowing Gideon, that a laugh like that was Gideon laughing at himself.

At the time that Gideon's mood changed so abruptly to laughter because Chamberlain had had to alter his plans, Chief Thwaites was in the Tate Gallery. Over a year before, Hogarth's "Boot Boy" had been stolen from the Tate, and had never been recovered. He, Thwaites, had not been in charge of the investigation, but now he wanted to learn exactly how the robbery had been achieved. The Assistant Director, Adam Charles, told him precisely, and Thwaites made mental notes to be written later in his reports.

No one at the gallery, except Charles, knew he was a policeman.

Leaving the Tate, Thwaites drove direct to the Victoria and Albert Museum, from which a Turner and two Constables had been stolen just two years before. Here, the Deputy Director was equally cooperative but could not help much. Thwaites made his notes and went back to the Yard, where he added them to the others already made, then tried to find a common factor in all the thefts. He failed, yet was feeling quite hopeful when- he left the Yard again, to go to Judd's place at Hampstead.

13: The Whispering Well

"Lance," Christine Falconer said, "are you *absolutely* sure you can trust Robin?"

"Christine, my love, I am absolutely sure I can trust Robin to do what he says he'll do, and so can you," Lancelot Judd answered. "I wish you weren't so doubtful. He hasn't done anything to upset you, has he?"

"No," answered Christine. "He always makes me feel uneasy, that's all. Tell me more about him."

"There isn't all that interesting to tell," said Lancelot. "We were at school together; we failed to get into the same university, but we met during vacations. We had thought of going into business together, since we both love antiques, but I stayed in England. Robin went to Canada and America to look for antique markets; he's always been interested in the subject. His father owned a wonderful collection of Japanese paintings and jade. I declared war on war, as you well know."

Christine half laughed.

"Did you really believe you could do any good, darling?"

"I believed it then," answered Lancelot rather ruefully. "But I don't really know what to make of things now. If you're in any doubt, I'm still as anti-war as ever; if there were a war tomorrow, I would be a conscientious objector, and if I thought it would do any good, I'd throw myself off a cliff crying *Outlaw war!*" He shifted his position slightly and slipped his right am firmly round her shoulders. It was Sunday morning; she was sitting on his knee in a huge armchair in his one-room studio flat above the Hampstead shop. "When did I last tell you that I loved you?"

"Too long ago," Christine answered.

He kissed her—

He kissed her in a way she had never known before, fiercely, demandingly, holding her tighter and still tighter. She felt the wild stirring of desire.

When, at last, he drew his head back, he was breathing very hard.

"I love you," he said. "I would love you whether you were a baker's daughter or a merchant banker's." He sounded both hoarse and urgent. "You know that, don't you?"

"Of *course* I know it," she answered. "Darling, *why* do you ask me so often?"

"Because I doubt you so often."

"Oh, Lance," she said helplessly. "You don't *need* to. I swear you don't need to. I can't help being a rich man's daughter. Sometimes I *hate* the thought of Daddy's money and all it does to him."

He bent his head and stopped her with another kiss, gentle this time. She moved her head back as if to get him into better perspective, and studied him for several moments without speaking.

"Why do you say you doubt me?" she asked, at last.

"Because you so often doubt my motives."

"I don't, you know. I really don't."

"Subconsciously you do," he told her. "I suppose the truth is you've been brainwashed since you were very young. You've been taught that no man could possibly love you for yourself alone, that anyone with a father as rich as yours is inevitably prey to get-rich-quick men. *Hush!* You were probably told this in the form of nursery rhymes first, and then the pressure was stepped up and you had a governess instead of going to school, so that you couldn't be contaminated with mere money seekers. *Quiet!* The excuse, of course, was that your parents travelled so much and wanted you with them, and they could afford your private tutors wherever you went. And you didn't realize what was happening and you don't realize what did happen, even today. You don't doubt me with your conscious mind but with your subconscious doubts."

"Lance, *please* stop!"

"No, darling, I won't stop; the time has come to talk. You *never* see Robin without doubting me, and—"

"But Robin's not you!"

"No. Robin, as you rightly say, is a long, long way from being me. But you think, or at least *fear,* he is using me to worm his way into your father's confidence. You haven't *really* worked the situation out in your mind, but you are as full of doubts as a font is full of holy water. I don't know how to exorcise those doubts, my sweet Christine. I really don't."

His arm was still around her, yet now she felt very different from the way she had felt only a few minutes before. Her heart was heavy and an unfamiliar tension gripped her.

"I can't help distrusting Robin," she said flatly.

"I'm not worried about Robin," he said. "I'm worried about—"

Before he added the word "you" and while he was pulling her even closer, a door banged downstairs in the shop.

"My God!" he exclaimed. "What's that?"

Although she tried to scramble off his lap quickly, it seemed an age before she was on her feet, and he pushed her aside so roughly as he stood up that she nearly stumbled. *"Stay there,"* he whispered, moving swiftly toward the door and the head of the narrow staircase. There was another sound from below, not so loud this time, and Lance raised his hand, then placed his finger on his lips, urging her to silence; and as she moved toward him he waved her away, mouthing: *"Stay there!"*

He looked terrified - not just alarmed, as she had been when the door banged, but terrified. He gripped the handrail tightly as he started silently down the stairs. Now no sound came from below. It was almost as if they had imagined the noises they had just heard.

Christine wondered what was frightening him so, and why it was so vital that she should stay where she was. For a few moments, until he disappeared, she stood close by the chair; but soon, drawn by curiosity, she moved toward the stairs. These were in fact little more than the open steps of a ladder, made of some dark, deeply polished wood, leading to a large apartment once part of a picture gallery, now used as living-room-cum-bedroom.

Christine's back was to the one wide window. The stairs were on her right. Alongside these were two doors, one leading to a W.C. and one to a tiny kitchen almost identical with those downstairs. There was a protective handrail, made of old brass curtain poles, gleaming in the brighter light which came up the well of the staircase.

A man out of sight said: "Is Robin—"

"*Hush!*" breathed Lance, whose back was all she could see. She noticed the twist of his lean body and knew that he was looking round and upward to see whether she was near, and instinctively she stepped back. This was the first time she had ever attempted to deceive Lance; it had seemed to her that the essence of their love was the absolute naturalness between them, the lack of all pretence.

Her heart thumped sickeningly because he was so afraid that she would overhear.

"Is he here?" the man whispered.

"No. What the hell made *you* come here?"

"I wanted to clarify a couple of matters," the other replied.

"Don't be a bloody fool, you didn't have to! My God, you're so hot you could set the bloody place on fire!"

Each word, trapped somewhere in the shop, travelled with soft clarity up the well of the staircase, and although the men were whispering they might almost have been standing by Christine's side. She moved nearer the kitchen door, where she could see more of the shop and yet be in less danger of being seen if they looked up. Now she could see the whole of Lance's body, except the top of his head, and she could see the stranger, sidewise to her, up as far as his chest. He wore a beige-coloured suit and beautifully polished brown shoes.

What did Lance mean by "You're so hot you could set the bloody place on fire?"

What did "hot" mean?

The very question was self-deceit. She knew, of course. No one who read or watched crime stories could be in any doubt and yet she did not want to believe that Lance was using the term so freely.

"I came because I no longer trust you, or Robin," the stranger said. "I think you're planning to keep all the money you get for it."

"It." What did he mean? What was "it?"

"Robin told you to—"

"Robin told me he could dispose of it in less than twelve hours," the other man said. He raised his voice very slightly, as if in anger. "Did you or did you not?" He spoke well but with slight over precision, and he sounded - the thought impinged itself on Christine's mind without making a deep impression - as if he were tired.

"Keep your voice down!" Lance said softly. "There—there was a delay. It wasn't our fault, there was a hitch. You'll get your money."

"I want to see either it or the money now," the man said flatly.

"What?"

"And I mean to have one or the other. Because I have to leave the country at once."

"Why? What's the hurry?"

"I am being watched."

"My God!" Lance gasped. "You're being watched and you come *here!*"

"I've already waited four days longer than I said I would. Lance—"

"Get out of here!"

"I will not go without one or the other," the caller said, and a touch of anger sounded in his voice˜. "After that, I'm through."

"Like hell you're through!" Lancelot paused, and Christine pressed back against the kitchen door trying to see the stranger more fully. At last, she succeeded. He was not as tall as Lance but was just as lean, with a long, rather delicate face. He wore a modern-shaped trilby hat with a narrow brim, and there was a not-quite-English look about him.

Lancelot's whisper, curiously magnified, echoed yet again.

"Go away. Go away and wait until—"

"No," the man said. "Not now. I won't wait. I don't trust you. If Robin hadn't killed the others, or fixed it, anyway—"

"Shut up!" Lancelot said in anguish, craning his neck right round, but obviously he could not see Christine, and could have no idea of the clarity with which every word they uttered travelled upward. "Get out, quick. I'll tell Robin and he'll come and pay you."

"You don't seem to understand me," the other said harshly. "The moment you committed murder, I was through with waiting."

He put his right hand beneath his jacket, fumbled for a moment, then drew out a small automatic pistol, while Christine watched as if turned to stone. She felt as if she were living through a nightmare. Soon, she thought, soon I shall wake up. There was no moment of walking.

"Put that away!" Lance gasped.

"Get me the picture," the stranger ordered flatly "Get it now - or give me the rest of the money. Fifty-one thousand pounds, plus what you took from the others."

"You know I can't—"

"Get it, now!" the stranger grated.

There was a pause, which dragged out for what seemed a long time. Then, slowly, deliberately, the stranger raised his gun until at last Lance muttered: "He—he'll kill you for this."

"If I don't kill him first," said the stranger. "Get it!"

Lance moved; Christine could hear furniture being shifted,

scraping on the floor. The man with the gun was watching something out of sight. Then, suddenly, Lance appeared with what seemed a roll of canvas and handed it to the caller, who put his gun away and took the canvas gently. Christine could not fail to notice the care with which he handled it, how his long and delicate fingers hovered for a few moments before he drew away.

"You won't get a penny," Lance whispered. "You'll never find a market!"

"But I will live," the other said, and turned - and as he turned he started violently and backed into Lance. Lance moved quickly, to avoid him. Now Christine could see both of them from the back, and sensed they were staring at something in or near the shop doorway.

She was at screaming pitch.

What could it be, who could it be? She heard the shop door and footsteps sound, and then the door closed. The man who had the canvas put his hand to his pocket, and pulled out a gun, but suddenly Lance moved and snatched the gun from his fingers, then sprang back out of reach. The strange thing was that Lance still seemed terrified. A man walked firmly toward the others, who stood as if petrified. Then Lance moved, seemed to square his shoulders.

"Good—good morning, Officer," he said huskily.

So it was a policeman!

Christine thought: Shot . . . murdered . . . killed . . . murdered . . . killed . . . policeman. And now the nightmare was even more vivid. The newcomer stopped in front of them and she could see the skirt of his tunic, the buttons, the buckle of his belt.

"So I fooled you," Robin Kell said, in his unmistakable voice, and there was the bite of sarcasm in the way he spoke. "If I'd been the McCoy and not a stage policeman, you would have had the handcuffs on you by now; you even *look* as guilty as hell. What are *you* doing here? I told you to stay under cover with the loot."

Suddenly, he broke off. There was a moment of utter silence

as he turned toward the man with the canvas. He seemed to see the gun in Lance's hand for the first time.

"What's going on?" he demanded roughly. "Come on, tell me."

"He—he came and demanded the rest of the money or—or the canvas," gasped Lance. "He says he's through. He had a gun, this gun. I had to give it to him." He drew a deep breath. "But I wasn't going to let him get away with it. I would have stopped him somehow."

Into the silence that followed, the stranger said: "I want the money, Robin - the whole seventy-five thousand. Or the picture. And I want one or the other *now.*"

He made it seem as if it were he, and not Lance, standing behind him, who held the gun.

14: The Onslaught of Fear

Only then did the truth crash upon Christine. And yet how *could* it be? The Velazquez, the picture that had become the sensation of London, the sensation of the land. Suddenly most of what she had heard dropped into place, and, keyed up though she had been before, she was now much more conscious of danger. The realization ran through her mind, turning thought to tumult, and she stood motionless, almost too fearful to breathe.

"So you do, do you?" Robin began, in a rough voice "Well—"

"He's been followed!" Lance blurted out. "We can't do anything to him. He's been followed by the police!"

"You told me that you would sell it in twelve hours and bring me the balance," the unknown man said quite calmly. "You did not tell me that you would murder Jenkins and Slater in cold blood, and you did not tell me that I would have to wait."

"The police are following him, I tell you," Lance cried, then turned his head and stared up the staircase.

"I said that the police were watching me," the stranger corrected. "If I take the picture, I will also take the risk." He moved toward the door - toward Robin - the canvas under his arm "Tell him it won't help to squeeze the trigger," he went on. "The gun isn't loaded." After a pause, he said, "Let me pass."

"You stay just where you are," Robin Kell said savagely. "Lance, why did you give him the canvas? My God, what a bloody fool you are!"

At that instant, upheaval came below.

The stranger made a darting move forward, Robin's hand descended on his arm, there was a choking scream, and the stranger staggered backward. As he thumped against a tall chest of drawers that rocked and rattled, Robin swept his other arm around and thrust Lance out of the way, then bounded up the stairs.

Halfway up, he saw Christine crouching back.

"I *thought* you were there," he said. "So now you know."

As he stopped and stared at her, lips tight and eyes glittering, she felt such an onslaught of terror that she could neither scream nor move. Robin seemed to stand there for an age, but it was only for a few seconds. Then he moved swiftly upward, vaulted over the handrail, gripped her hand, and spun her round, pushing her arm high up behind her, making pain streak through her elbow and her shoulder. He seemed to do everything in a series of movements that were part of one another, opening the door of the W.C. and thrusting her inside, letting her arm go, and then, while terror welled up and she felt as if her lungs would burst she wanted so desperately to scream, he brought the side of his hand onto the back of her neck in a savage chopping blow. Her head jolted backward, her neck felt as if it were breaking. She lost consciousness and slumped against the wall.

Robin Kell stepped out of the tiny closet, the key in his hand. He put it into the keyhole from the outside, turned it, and, when the lock had clicked, withdrew the key and dropped it into his pocket. Then he turned round to see Lancelot Judd staring at him from halfway up the stairs.

"You—you didn't hurt her, did you?"

"I just put her to sleep."

"If you've hurt her—"

"Look out!" exclaimed Robin. "I'm coming!" He placed a hand on the cold brass rail and vaulted, and Lance only just dodged to one side in time. Down below, sitting on a high-backed Jacobean chair, the other man - de Courvier - was nursing his arm. As Robin appeared, he got up and turned slowly toward the door, but he was obviously so sick with pain that he could walk only a few steps, and those swaying.

"Come back, Paul," Robin ordered.

Paul de Courvier took an unsteady pace forward.

"Come back, or I'll break the other arm," Robin said through his teeth.

De Courvier stopped and slowly turned round. His right arm was twisted where it had been broken, and all the colour had drained out of his face. His eyes looked feverishly bright, and his thin lips were set tightly.

"When did you last see the police watching?" Robin demanded.

"At—at my flat," the other answered.

"Are you sure they were watching you?"

"They followed—followed me twice."

"Have they been to see you?"

"No."

"Haven't broken in when you've been out, have they?"

"No, there's been no sign of a search," de Courvier muttered. "I—I must go to a hospital. My arm—"

"You just answer my questions," Robin Kell said callously. "How did you come here?"

"I borrowed someone's car."

"Borrowed?"

"A neighbour's. He's away."

"Are you sure he's away?"

"Of course I am sure! And we have an arrangement; we use each other's cars sometimes. If you let me go now, I won't talk. If you keep me here, I'll tell the police everything, when they come." De Courvier's voice was thick with pain.

"Shut up! What car is your neighbour's?"

"A white Jaguar. I tell you—"

"What's all this about being through?" Robin interrupted harshly.

"I—I *am* through. I don't want anything more to do with the job. Can't you understand?"

"You can't get away with it so easily," Robin said, sneering. "You'll do exactly what I tell you."

"No!" de Courvier said, "I will do nothing more for you or with you. You lie about everything, and you kill without compunction. There was no need to murder Jenkins and Slater. There was no need to lie to me. Now you have your portrait, and if you really have a buyer you can keep my share of the money. I am finished. There is nothing you can do to make me—"

De Courvier broke off, and caught his breath, then seemed to hiss. Robin Kell moved with his remarkable ease and precision, hand going to his waistband, sliding out, blade of a knife glinting, then, with a swift movement, burying itself in de Courvier's belly. And as he died, and swayed backward, Robin held his shoulders to keep him upright.

Without looking round, he said: "We'll get rid of him after dark."

Behind him, Lancelot Judd gasped, "You're a cold-blooded swine."

"Let's just say I'm cold-blooded," Robin retorted, and he half dragged the dead man behind a big wardrobe, almost too large for the shop, and propped him up on another high-backed chair.

"If you hurt Christine—"

"Don't be a fool," Robin interrupted. "We *need* Christine. You can have her for bed. I want her because she'll open a lot of doors in Falconer House. If we handle this properly, and we're going to, we'll separate Falconer from most of his money. But we need Christine alive to do that."

Lance began, "You mean—"

"I mean we're on our way to a fortune. Falconer would be tempted like hell to buy the Velazquez anyhow. When he knows that buying it is the only way to save his daughter from drugs and shall we say degradation, he'll fall over himself to buy it. And, oh boy," - an expression of unbelievable cunning spread over Robin Kell's face, making him look quite demonic - "oh, *boy,*" he repeated in a low-pitched voice, "won't we have him where we want him then? He'll buy everything we want him to, or the police will be tipped off to pay him a visit."

Lance was watching him, appalled, but as if mesmerized. Robin's tone changed.

"So we're home and dry. All we have to do is keep our heads. There were only three men who *could* have caused us any real trouble, but now they can't. We've got to work out how to get rid of the body. The best way will be to get de Courvier back in the Jaguar. It doesn't matter where it's found; the trusting neighbour will report it stolen and the police will think it all happened in the car."

He nodded to himself with obvious satisfaction.

"So long as you don't hurt Christine," Lance said weakly.

"I won't hurt Christine if she behaves herself," Robin said absently "It's past time we put this piece of lolly away, now. My God! You could have got us into real trouble!" But he did not dwell on that, only raised the Velazquez shoulder high and stepped toward a wall adjoining the next-door building, on which several big paintings, none of any quality, hung from a picture rail. "Come and lend a hand," he added more brusquely.

Lance moved after him, and together they took the pictures down. Then Robin pressed a section of the rail, and the now bare wall slid open, revealing a dark recess beyond, about three or four feet deep. Inside were a dozen cylindrical metal containers, each marked "Fire Resistant." Robin picked one up from the left-hand side, twisted a key in a small lock, opened the hinged top, and turned toward Lance, who was rolling the Velazquez. Taking the picture, he eased it gently into the container and then closed the cap. He tested it to make sure the self-locking device worked, then put it with those on the right-hand side.

"Eleven in the bag," he remarked. "We won't worry about making it a round dozen." He pressed the picture rail again and the doors slid to; then they put the pictures back.

"Foolproof and fireproof," Robin observed "We're nearer that fortune than we've ever been. And no one can give us away now - all of them are dead."

Lancelot Judd nodded, but almost at once gave an involuntary shiver. Robin appeared not to notice. Neither of them spoke of Christine.

"Did you know that Christine wouldn't be in for lunch?" asked Sir Richard Falconer. He was lunching, frugally for him, in the morning room overlooking the walled garden of Falconer House, a garden with a centuries-old lawn, smooth as velvet, bordered on one side by espalier apple and pear trees, still heavy with fruit, and on the other by the rich variety of colours and blooms of late dahlias and early chrysanthemums.

"Yes, I knew," Lady Falconer answered.

"Do you know where she intended to go?"

"With Lancelot Judd, of course."

"It's *very* risky, Charlotte," Falconer said severely.

"It's even more risky for us to try to live her life for her," retorted his wife, with rare spirit. "If you restrict her too much, she will rebel completely and leave home."

"I don't think you know her as well as I do." Falconer cut a piece off a peach and placed it in his mouth. "She will accept - she *does* accept - the situation, and she will certainly not be foolish enough to leave home. Life in a garret or what passes for penury these days certainly would not suit her, nor will this young man. Do you *really* know anything about him?"

"I know you have no doubt set your spies on him," Lady Falconer said bitterly.

"Charlotte, I really don't understand you. I must take the obvious precautions. Of course I needed to check the background of Lancelot Judd, who might possibly have proved suitable as an escort for Christine. He is the son of Jacob Judd, a Brighton solicitor; got a scholarship to Oxford, and worked in an antique shop during vacations, so he has some knowledge of antiques and paintings. But until he set up shop he lived on a small inheritance, and seems to be a somewhat odd young man. He was very active in the Campaign for Nuclear Disarmament, a campaign which you know that I abominated. And he has friends who are no less odd. Christine must be persuaded to break the association."

His wife looked at him out of her beautiful shell, and her voice carried more feeling than her features - even her eyes - showed.

"Christine is extremely resentful at being watched and followed wherever she goes. You *must* stop doing that, and give her her head for a while."

Falconer toyed delicately with another sliver of peach.

"I must at least appear to," he conceded, "and I made a start only this morning. I told Oily not to have anyone follow her today. But if she isn't back for dinner I shall regret it very much indeed."

"She'll be back," his wife said with assurance. "She promised to be here for dinner." She relaxed a little as the footman brought in coffee: on Sundays they always had coffee in this room. As she poured, she smiled at her husband, and when she passed the tiny cup of priceless porcelain, their hands touched for a moment in a kind of aloof intimacy.

Gideon, on that pleasant Sunday afternoon, hoed vigorously among the late-summer flowers in the back garden and, when the rich earth had been stirred, took a pair of edging shears from the small garden shed and began to trim the lawn edges. Insects kept perching on his face and he brushed them off with the back of his hand. Now and again, when he stopped, he could hear the piano; Penelope was practising as if her very life were at stake. Kate was upstairs, getting ready to go out; they were going to supper with Prudence, the eldest daughter, her husband, and their five-year-old child. It would be pleasant but not exciting; like the gardening.

Gardening soothed Gideon, and while he gardened he was

able to think clearly without fogging his mind by too much concentration. Often, while pottering with lengths of bass, or with secateurs, tidying the shed or adjusting the blades on the lawnmower, he had flashes of illumination on matters which might have been worrying him for days. Today was mostly ruminative. He couldn't do any more about the National Gallery inquiry and hadn't yet made up his mind whether to attend the conference on Tuesday morning, or whether to delegate Hobbs. He wondered where Riddell was, thought of the dead Pakistani girl. Was hers an isolated case or did such things happen often? If a conference was needed, it was over the immigrant smuggling, but that was a major social problem, not simply one for the police, and he had a sense of the need for caution.

He couldn't consult Chamberlain; the man would be impossible. Nor did he want to handle this on his own. The only person to discuss the problem with was Sir Reginald Scott-Marie, the Commissioner. Perhaps this evening he would call him; it would be easier to discuss it out of office hours, and Scott-Marie could be trusted absolutely.

He wondered how Entwhistle was, and whether Honiwell was right, and the case could and should be reopened. Was it really possible that Greenwood had let Entwhistle spend three years in prison, to face the rest of his life in prison, for a crime he hadn't committed? What went on in the minds of such men? How could anybody live with a burden like that on his conscience?

The simple truth was, of course, that such men had no conscience, it was a hard thing to accept, and although Gideon had been dealing with the most ruthless and hardened criminals all his life, it was still difficult for him, especially on a Sunday afternoon in the garden, to believe that men could be so cold-blooded. But suddenly he had a revulsion of feeling against his own thinking. He knew damned well that some men were so utterly coldblooded that they did not have a spark of remorse or contrition whatever they did.

The killer of Jenkins, the killer of Slater might well be cases in point.

There was a furious burst of music, a moment of praise and triumph; bless the child! He wondered how the strange *affaire* between her and Hobbs was progressing. She appeared most of the time to regard Hobbs as an uncle or an elder brother, and though she sometimes seemed almost to be in love with him, such periods did not last long. Soon she would meet another, younger man with whom, for a few weeks, sometimes only for a few days, she would be completely infatuated.

Odd not to know how one's children thought and felt. The parent-child relationship was a strange one, and often totally unpredictable. Take for example Jenkins and his daughter Lucy.

Funny about Lucy, working in a shop that he, Gideon, passed every day. He had read the report from the Division at Fulham; it had been written with a rare sensitivity which had somehow made him understand Lucy's reaction to her father's death. The tragedy wasn't in the death but in the revelation of the estrangement between father and daughter. Funny, too, about that yearly Christmas card with a five-pound note tucked inside.

He had only a few feet of the lawn edge to finish when he heard Kate from the window.

"George!"

The piano was still playing, a neighbour's lawnmower was clattering.

"George! Telephone!" Kate was mouthing the words and beckoning.

A little reluctantly, Gideon put down the shears and strolled into the kitchen. There was an extension in the passage just outside the door. The music ended, by chance or with intent, and he picked up the receiver.

"Gideon here."

"I'm sorry to worry you on Sunday afternoon, George," said Sir Reginald Scott-Marie, "but I would like a word with you about Tuesday's conference. Can you fit it in sometime this evening without disturbing your family too much?"

He could!

"About half past nine tonight, sir, if that would suit you," Gideon replied promptly.

"Make it ten o'clock, will you? We needn't be too long. Thank you. Goodbye."

Gideon rang off, smiling with deep satisfaction. Scott-Marie must have sensed what Chamberlain had been doing, and deliberately relieved Gideon of the need to broach the subject. Yet Scott-Marie had a reputation for being the most coldly aloof man at the Yard. Ten o'clock was easier, really; he could bring Kate and Penelope home and then go to Scott-Marie's place in Mayfair.

It couldn't be better.

On the other side of London, above Lancelot Judd's little shop, Christine Falconer lay in a drugged sleep.

Barely half a mile away from Gideon, at the back of Old Fisky's shop, Lucy Jenkins watched the old man as he worked on her possible find. She could hardly control her impatience, her longing for a dream to come true.

15: The Find

Old Fisky did what Lucy had done at first, placed the picture flat on the bench, the odds and ends of rags, bottles, pieces of frame, glasses, brushes, cigarette packets, and empty matchboxes pushed to one side. Then he soaked a rag in turpentine, using far more than she would have dared to, and smeared it over the canvas, peering at it with sharp, unblinking eyes while the little miracle occurred. As the turpentine made the dirt and the varnish beneath it translucent, the picture itself began to show up. He grunted but made no comment, allowed the turpentine to dry, and then repeated the process. This time, he picked the wet picture up and held it so that the light shone on it. Clear, sunless light from the north, pure as light could be, made the three partly draped figures look very real.

"It's certainly odd," he said. "Varnish is very cracked. Put that diacetate nearer and get me some more cotton wool." Under his breath he muttered something which sounded like "You should know what I want by now."

But Lucy was too excited to feel rebuked.

Old Fisky picked up a paintbrush with the hairs almost completely worn away, took the cotton wool Lucy handed him, and wound it round the thick end of the brush until it was a cylindrical shape about the size of a cigarette. Lucy pushed a bottle marked "diacetate" toward him, and unscrewed the plastic cap. He dipped the stick inside, held it for a moment to soak the cotton wool, then allowed the excess liquid to drip back into the bottle before moving it to another corner of the picture. Slowly, he drew it across the canvas, and it took the dirt away as if by magic. He dabbed the cloth soaked in turpentine on the clean patch, then repeated the process until a strip about a quarter inch wide ran for three inches across the painting. Vivid blue and dull white showed up.

"It's dry enough now," he said. "Give me my glass, girl - for heaven's sake, don't just stand there."

Without a word, Lucy handed him a magnifying glass about the size of a small saucer. She was unable to stop herself from trembling, because his manner told her that he was as excited as she was. He peered through the glass, now close to the cleaned strip, now a few inches away, and when he drew back he handed her the glass.

"Have a look for yourself . . . See what I mean when I talk of *craquelure* - those tiny, tiny cracks . . . Oh, it's *old.*" She was hardly able to hold the glass still, excitement so possessed her. "Depends on the kind of varnish, of course, but at least three hundred years old, I would say, and Dutch. You only get that kind of blue in Dutch paintings – a secret they kept to themselves, never been able to reproduce it. Can you *see?*"

She could see the vivid blue of the paint and the myriad criss-cross lines where the varnish had cracked with dryness and age. It seemed to her that she had never seen so pure a blue, and she knew that Old Fisky was enraptured by it. The tiny criss-cross of cracks in the varnish was unmistakable, too. He had told her of this but she had never seen it so clearly before.

He took the glass from her, his hands spotted and with the veins standing out, hers very small and delicate and white.

"Now we will take it off the new canvas," he said. "Anyone who saw the new canvas and the paint on it would think the dirt was new, wouldn't give It a second thought. Except you!" He cackled to himself as he filled a big sink with water and put in a little detergent which would not affect the paint or the varnish but would soak the new canvas until it became loose and could be pulled away. After allowing the picture to float for ten minutes, he examined it with infinite care; then he pushed his few locks of hair back, and looked at Lucy with his head on one side.

"It's an old one, Lucy, you can be sure of that. We'll leave it for half an hour; the two canvases will pull apart easily then. How about me making you a cup of tea, for a change; it's Sunday, and Martha's out at church." He turned toward the stairs, and thumped heavily up them, Lucy following him. "Warm today," he remarked, loosening his collar.

"I'll make it," she said

She went into the kitchen and made the tea, as they both knew she would, then cut a few slices of his favourite wholemeal bread, spreading it with butter so soft that it melted into the coarse grain.

He was sitting in a big old saddleback chair, feet up on a pouffe, huge boots jutting out like boats. As she came in with the tray, he tapped the stool by his side.

"Put it here, I'll pour out."

She laid the tray on the stool and drew up a small sewing chair, one she especially liked because it gave her arms and elbows freedom. Old Fisky handed her a cup.

"You're a very good girl, Lucy, and I know I'm an old grouch sometimes, but you're a very good girl. You don't try to do what you're not qualified for, and that's unusual in a young woman. You'll be rewarded one of these days, don't worry about that."

"Do you think this *is* a find?" she asked eagerly.

"It's an old picture," he repeated noncommittally. He poured a cup for himself. "I'm sorry about your father, Lucy," he went on unexpectedly.

She closed her eyes but didn't speak.

"Don't you ever feel lonely?" Old Fisky asked.

"Yes," she admitted. "Yes, sometimes."

"Never thought of getting married?"

She opened her eyes wide in astonishment.

"Don't be daft," she said flatly.

"But that's not daft," he protested. "Don't you like men,

Lucy?"

"I never think of them," she stated simply.

"If you did your hair properly, and if you—" He broke off, drank his tea in great gulps, and immediately poured himself another cup. "Oh, never mind, never mind. It's your own life, as Martha keeps reminding me." He was mumbling now, talking to himself, and Lucy could barely distinguish the words. "Make yourself attractive and some fellow will come and take you off, and I'll lose the best assistant I ever had." Suddenly, much louder, he asked, "Will you have more tea?"

"Yes, please," she said meekly.

At last the half hour passed, and on the tick of the last minute Old Fisky stood up and led the way downstairs. Side by side, they looked at the picture and saw that it was still floating; then Fisky pulled it out of the water and held it up gingerly by that magic corner. There were bubbles in the new canvas; the new and the old were coming apart. Now he laid it, painted side down, on an old towel, and began to pull the two pieces apart. He kept picking pieces off his fingers, the old paste used in the relining, hardened by the years but soft after half an hour of soaking.

"It's just relined," he said "That cleaning label was a fake. Now, let's dry it out and see if we can see what it is." She waited, only too aware of her own shortcomings, while he examined the picture.

Soon appeared larger patches of the blue and white and then other, richer colours, reds, greens and yellows and pinks of the flesh and browns of hair and eyes. The old man breathed very hoarsely; there was no doubt at all of his excitement.

"I think it's a John Bettes - that's sixteenth-century Dutch," he said. "Let me have the Benezit, Volume Three. Hurry, girl, hurry!" Lucy turned to the wall shelf where the row of green bound books stood, took down the volume he wanted, and held it out to him. He flipped over page after page, then suddenly stopped.

He glanced at her over the rims of his glasses and she did not know what was in his mind, but he had discovered something. He beckoned her and she joined him, feeling almost sick with hope and apprehension. His long forefinger was pointing at a black-and-white plate, and she saw at a glance that this was a picture of the painting she had found - and she also knew, from Old Fisky's manner, that this wasn't all it seemed to be.

"What is it?" she gasped. "Please, what is it?"

" 'Summer Idyll'," Old Fisky said slowly. "It was stolen from Rosebury House in Suffolk about ten years ago. It's a find all right, Lucy, it's a big find; it's a very valuable painting. And" - he put a damp hand on her shoulder, and went on in a gentle voice - "there'll be a reward, my dear, quite a substantial reward."

"Mr. Fisk," she asked, hardly breathing, "How *much* would you think? Please tell me how much."

He looked at her, moistened his lips, and then said, "Fifty pounds, at least, fifty pounds - it might even be a hundred."

And he knew, as anyone would have known who saw the rapturous expression on her face, that she was enthralled, that to her a hundred or even fifty pounds would be a fortune.

He had never seen her looking so happy.

Nor had Police Constable Wilberforce, who "happened" to be passing on the other side of the road when, an hour later, she went out for a walk. He was not in uniform, so he could follow her without being too obvious, and he walked along King's Road and then into New King's Road and across to the Eelbrook Common, where many played and more strolled and sunned themselves in the lovely evening. Lucy walked as she always did toward Walham Green, now known to many as Fulham Broadway, and he cut along another path, easily outpacing her, until near the Broadway he was able to turn and walk toward her, so that soon they came face to face.

His eyes brightened and he managed to sound surprised.

"Why, Miss Jenkins!"

She looked puzzled as he drew up.

"Don't you recognize me?" he asked "Wilberforce, P.C.

Wilberforce. I saw you on Wednesday, when I came to the shop."

"Oh, I remember!" She was quite pleased. "You had your uniform on then, so I didn't recognize you."

"That's easy to understand," he said "Are you going far?"

"Just for a walk, that's all"

"May I join you?" Ian Wilberforce asked.

"Well—well, yes, that would be very nice." Lucy's eyes lit up in turn, and there was a new brightness in her as they walked back toward New King's Road, then along the terraced houses which flanked one side of the common, and eventually to Parsons Green. When they were there, he asked, as if out of a brain wave: "It's a lovely evening - would you like to take a bus up to Putney and walk along the river?"

"I'd love it!" she cried. But suddenly her voice plummeted in dismay: "But if I'm taking up too much of your time—"

"Not a bit," he said hurriedly. "It's my day off, and I'm as free as the air. Days off are a bit boring sometimes," he went on. "I live in digs, you see, and it's hardly home from home."

They sat close together on the bus.

They linked arms on the towpath. They walked slowly, very slowly, back toward the bus, two hours later.

I daren't kiss her, he thought, it would scare the wits out of her. She's as fragile as a bird.

He's wonderful, she thought, he's wonderful, but I hope he doesn't want to kiss me. I'd faint if he wanted to kiss me.

"Goodbye," he said. "I've enjoyed being with you so much."

"Oh, so have I!"

"If you're free on my next day off, perhaps—perhaps we could go to the pictures."

"Oh" she said, her heart in her voice. "I'd *love to*."

That was a little after half past seven, and at the very moment when Lucy was closing the front door of the shop in Fulham, Sir Richard Falconer was opening the door of his wife's bedroom, a long and immaculate Regency room with a canopy over the head of the bed. Beyond, opposite the main door, was the bathroom and a tiny dressing room.

Lady Falconer came out of the dressing room, and started at the sight of him.

If he was aware that it was the first time he had been in her room for nearly a year, he gave no sign. He was dressed in a dark suit and a tie with a single pearl pin, and the pearl picked out the colour of the hair at his temples; he was a little thinner than he had been for some time past, and there was more animation in him than he had allowed his wife to see for years.

"Charlotte, has Christine telephoned?" he demanded.

"No."

"Are you quite sure? Could your maid have forgotten a message?"

"I've been in all the afternoon," Charlotte Falconer answered. "I'm as worried as—" She paused for a fraction, and then went on: "As you are."

"Are you sure she was going out with this man Judd?"

"She didn't say so," his wife replied. "She simply said that she must have a life of her own, that she wasn't going to have lunch with us but was going out."

"So you only assumed she would see Judd?"

"Yes, Richard. But, knowing her, I can't think I am wrong."

"No," mused Falconer "You're almost certainly right, of course. I'm *very* worried, Charlotte."

"Yes," Charlotte said, almost wonderingly. "I can see you are. But, Richard—" She paused again because he looked so impatient, but went on to say exactly what she had intended to say: "It isn't a catastrophe or a crisis because a young woman of twenty-three goes out to lunch and stays out to dinner, you know."

Falconer caught his breath.

"I am quite aware of that. I am also aware of my daughter's character. She went out to lunch, and told you, so that you should not be anxious. Not because she felt any obligation - she is obviously in a mood of revolt against me - but because she would not wish to hurt you." He astonished Charlotte by his positiveness, by the evidence that he knew Christine's nature and temperament remarkably well. "And she would not say she would be home for dinner unless she meant to be."

"She could have changed her mind."

"Then she would have telephoned."

"She might not be near a telephone."

"Then she is in a very peculiar place." Falconer hesitated, studied his wife closely and much as he would one of his other precious possessions, and then said in a more subdued voice: "If she isn't here by half past nine, I shall ask the police to search for her. Meanwhile, I shall tell Oily to send someone to the shop in Hampstead." He went out, and she heard a rare and remarkable thing: his voice, *raised*. "Oily!" There were sounds of footsteps, and then Oliphant's voice sounded in turn.

"At once, Richard . . ."

". . . And I want to know the result whatever they find, whatever I am doing," Falconer finished. "If you must, interrupt me at dinner."

Oliphant's voice carried back faintly: "You shall hear the moment there is any news."

Two men went to the shop in Hampstead Village, tried the front door, and rang the bell. No one answered. No one appeared to be in the shop. They left, passing a Jaguar which gleamed very white beneath a street lamp. As they went, Robin Kell watched from a corner of the first floor window.

"There's no answer," Oliphant reported to Falconer soon afterward.

It was then ten minutes past nine.

"Who do you think it was?" asked Lance Judd huskily.

"Sir Flicking Richard Falconer's leg men," growled Robin Kell.

"Are you - are you sure it wasn't the police?"

"I'm sure," Robin said. "And let me tell you this. Rather than let the cops or anyone else get those paintings without paying for them, I'd burn the lot. Don't make any mistake, I'd burn the lot. If they're no use to me, they won't be any use to anyone."

Lancelot Judd felt quite sure he meant exactly what he said.

16: The Commissioner

At half past nine, Gideon took a surreptitious glance at his watch, then pretended he was absolutely absorbed in the singing and the playing - as, but for Scott-Marie, he would have been. From the moment he and Kate had arrived, everything had gone with a swing. Penelope had arrived soon afterward with her latest conquest, a youth named Peter, Hobbs apparently forgotten. Prudence's husband, another Peter had obviously taken to him; the five-year-old grandchild found first Kate's lap and then Gideon's shoulder places of comfort. Kate had gone into the front room of the little suburban house and started to strum on the piano. Kate's playing was of the Sunday School teacher type, accurate but very deliberate. Penny's Peter had produced a harmonica and begun to play with a practised ease. Prudence had pulled her violin from behind the upright piano and, for no reason at all, had started an Irish jig which everyone followed. Gideon and Pru's Peter had found themselves in the kitchen, carving cold joints, then laying the dining-room table, and "dinner" had been a running buffet to the liveliest musical accompaniment.

Gideon had known occasions when he would have found such an evening raucous and off-putting, but tonight he was as nearly content as a man could be. And now Penelope was to play her sonata and Prudence, playing the violin as well as in her orchestra days, was to follow with a piece by Liszt. And in half an hour Gideon was due at the Commissioner's home, half an hour's drive away. He hadn't said anything to Kate, expecting the party to break up about nine o'clock, as it usually did.

Just before Penny began, the front doorbell rang, and Pru's Peter slipped away.

"Probably neighbours, to complain about the noise," Prudence gasped in mock horror. She was the most beautiful of Gideon's three daughters, and marriage and motherhood had warmed that beauty. "It couldn't be anyone for *you,* Daddy, could it?"

Gideon pulled a face while his heart leapt hopefully. Peter came back, a tall, young-looking man with a shock of curly hair. He raised both hands to enjoin silence, and when it fell he said sepulchrally: *"The cops!"*

It was an evening when such a crack was hilariously funny, and they all roared. As Gideon followed Peter out, he caught Kate's eyes and recognized her expression: *You knew you'd be called out, didn't you?* On the porch a uniformed policeman was standing almost at attention, and at the curb stood a police car, blue sign glowing.

"Commander Gideon?"

"Yes."

"Sorry to disturb you, but there is an urgent message on walkie-talkie for you, sir."

Gideon, who had already made up his mind what to do, slipped the keys of his own car into his son-in-law's hand, and said huskily: "Happiest evening I've had for a long time, Peter. I won't break it up. Will you ask Mother to drive home? I'll get there as soon as I can."

"Right-ho," said Peter. "It *has* been good, hasn't it?"

"I tell you, my happiest evening for a long time. I haven't seen the family so much together for years." Gideon gripped Peter's hand, then went off down the short drive, the uniformed man a pace behind him. The other patrol man was standing by the side of the car, walkie-talkie in his hand.

"One of you get in the back; I'll sit next to the driver," Gideon said. "I want you to drive me somewhere in a hurry." He flicked on the walkie-talkie and announced: "Gideon," and squeezed into the car. "Drive toward central London, will you?"

"Sorry to disturb you, sir," a man said on the walkie-talkie as the car started off smoothly. Everyone was a sight too solicitous tonight. "This is Thwaites. A man was found in the seat of a Jaguar car in a garage at a block of flats in Swiss Cottage tonight - twenty minutes or so ago, as a matter of fact."

"Well?" Gideon said.

"Positively identified as Paul de Courvier, who lived at the flats," Thwaites said. "I picked up some conclusive evidence that de Courvier and Jenkins were working with Slater on some unknown job, and I was going to report first thing in the morning. *Three* of them are dead now. I thought you ought to know at once, sir."

"You're quite right," said Gideon. "Where's the body?"

"Still in the car, sir."

"Finish what has to be done and then get it to the morgue at the Yard," Gideon ordered. "How long had the body been there?"

"Only a short while. It's a long story, sir; the thing I rang you about is that Division says it was parked most of the day in - the Jaguar I mean, sir - was parked in Hampstead Village near Lancelot Judd's shop. And Judd is the boyfriend of Sir Richard Falconer's daughter, you'll remember. I thought you ought to know," Thwaites repeated. "I'm having the movements of the car traced."

"Was it stolen?"

"No, sir, I don't think - it really *is* a bit complicated to explain over the telephone." Thwaites was actually pleading with Gideon to say he would go straight to the spot. This in itself was unusual. Thwaites knew better than to expect the Commander to go out on any job; that was why he was being careful not to make the suggestion.

"I'll be in my office in about an hour: say, an hour and a half," Gideon said "Call me there."

If Thwaites felt any disappointment, he hid it successfully.

"Very good, sir."

Gideon rang off, and looked round at the man behind him. The car was moving at a steady speed, the driver obviously very aware of his high-ranking passenger.

"Who's in charge in your division?" Gideon asked.

"Superintendent Loss, sir."

"Ask him if you can take me to Peel Crescent, Mayfair, and drop me there," Gideon said.

"Ask—" the man echoed, and then he stopped himself, reached for the radio, and spoke to his division. Formalities over, Gideon sat back in his seat, and after a few minutes, declared: "I'm in a hurry."

"Right, sir!" exclaimed the driver, and the car surged forward through the nearly empty streets. Rain began to fall softly, making the road surfaces greasy, but Gideon was thinking back to the liveliness of the evening, the happiness; and he gave little thought to what Thwaites had said and why Thwaites had been so anxious to talk to him. Then the car pulled up outside a house in a crescent terrace of Georgian houses which had a peaceful stateliness even in the lamplight diffused by rain that was now falling steadily but softly. The car drove off on its patrols, wheels swishing, and when it had disappeared the only sound was the soft pattering rain. It was ten minutes past ten, and he could recall the time when his heart would have been in his mouth because he had kept the Commissioner waiting. There was a light inside a wrought-iron shade above the fan-shaped light over the door. Gideon pressed the bell, and almost immediately footsteps sounded.

Sir Reginald Scott-Marie opened the door himself.

"Ah. Come in, George." The "George", was clear evidence that he meant this to be informal. "What, no coat?" They entered the hall, with the staircase and its polished balustrade leading upward; the walls were duck-egg blue, the lighting subdued; several portraits, all of Scott-Marie's ancestors, hung on the wall. If there was an ideal house in Gideon's mind, this was it.

Scott-Marie led the way into a study-cum-library, with a big desk, book-lined walls, rich carpet, deep and comfortable-looking armchairs. Between these was a table with two decanters and four glasses.

"Brandy?" suggested Scott-Marie.

"Thank you." Gideon, sitting, looked up at the tall, lean man with the close-cut grey hair and the clipped moustache, the slightly sandy complexion, the chilling grey eyes. This man had become a legend in the Metropolitan Police Force; a martinet who nevertheless knew and was considerate of people, whoever they were.

Scott-Marie poured brandy into two bowl shaped glasses, and sat down. A glow came from a single-bar electric fire, slightly incongruous in the Adam fireplace.

"How much do you know about the conference due on Tuesday morning?" Scott-Marie asked, and implied very much more them the words themselves.

Gideon said mildly, "I've been informed."

Scott-Marie obviously appreciated the dryness of that comment. He sniffed the brandy, and asked: "Would it serve any useful purpose if I were there?"

"It could serve one very good purpose," answered Gideon promptly.

"Exactly what?"

"There is a strong tendency to see the National Gallery theft as a London concern only," Gideon said. "It's much wider than that, of course, and I think we should extend the inquiries into all the provincial centres, as well as immediately ask for cooperation abroad. Customs officers could be of great help: a picture of this size, rolled or flat, wouldn't be easy to hide even on a cursory inspection. If you made it clear that you regard it both as a national and an international matter, then I think a lot of people will be suitably impressed."

"I see," said Scott-Marie.

Another man might have said: "Why isn't it being treated like that already?" And another man than Gideon would have said: "The Assistant Commissioner doesn't see it this way." Neither spoke, until at last Scott-Marie stretched his legs nearer the fire.

"I see," he said again. "I shall be at the conference."

"I thought I'd send Hobbs, sir," Gideon remarked.

Scott-Marie looked at him very directly, and he wondered whether a direct question was coming; but the moment passed, and the Commissioner sipped again before going on: "There's another thing I've been wanting to talk to you about for a long time, George."

And he now regarded the time as right, reflected Gideon.

"Yes, sir?"

"The smuggling of immigrants and the relationship between coloured people and the police generally," Scott-Marie said, and his lips turned down in a droll smile. "I know that's a tall order, but I'm concerned with the principles, not the detail. Are you satisfied with one, or the other, or both?"

"I'm not satisfied at all," Gideon answered quietly, "but I think the first will work itself out." He explained briefly about Riddell and what he planned, and then went on more firmly: "The relationship is a very different matter, sir. It's a question of individual reaction and the ruling circumstances. I've no evidence at all of a deteriorating relationship. But that isn't to say that it's good enough. I'm talking about our area, of course, and we have one or two difficult places, such as Notting Hill. It's so much more than a police matter."

"And yet we can exert a lot of influence," Scott-Marie observed. "I've just been to Scarborough, as you know. Reports about most of the matters discussed were given to the newspapers, but some were confidential. And among those not told to the press is the growing anxiety about the conditions and the situation caused by immigration. There is strong feeling that it isn't being handled very well by anybody."

Gideon made no comment.

"I was asked - as was every Chief Constable present - to investigate the local situation from the police point of view."

Gideon stirred uncomfortably.

"That's all right provided it's understood that the police *is* only one point of view, sir. There's a tendency in the press—" He broke off.

"Go on," urged Scott-Marie.

"A tendency to make us the scapegoats," said Gideon. "It's one thing for us to have a problem like the smuggling, which overlaps with social and industrial aspects; it's quite another for us to be regarded as the only people responsible. And there *is* that tendency, sir."

"Yes," agreed Scott-Marie. "There were some delegates at the conference who know this and resent it very much. I think I would like to discuss it with you, Riddell, and those Superintendents of Divisions where there is a larger-than-average proportion of coloured immigrants. While it's a long-term problem, there are short-term dangers, so I ought to do this fairly soon. When will Riddell be back?"

"In three weeks, sir."

"Then we'll set the date a month from now; check with my secretary, will you? Brief the Divisional men and Honiwell, and a few days before the conference - those conferences! - let me have a written assessment. Then you and I can talk about it the day before, say."

"I'll arrange all that," Gideon said. There was something else he wanted to say, but he wasn't sure this was the time. And he was tempted to tell Scott-Marie about Thwaites's suspicion of Sir Richard Falconer, but as it was only suspicion and not yet strongly based, he decided not to.

"Some doubt in your mind?" asked Scott-Marie.

"I'd like Hobbs to be with us at all stages, sir, unless you've any objection," Gideon answered.

"None," said Scott-Marie.

"And—" Gideon hesitated again, and did not feel very pleased with himself, but he had gone too far now, and went on: "Shall I brief the Assistant Commissioner, sir?"

"I will inform him," Scott-Marie said, in a more formal tone than he had used before.

"Thank you, sir." Gideon finished his brandy, then straightened up in his chair. "I really ought to be going, unless there's something else urgent. I promised to look in at the Yard before going home. Something had cropped up just before I started out, and I don't know the significance of it yet." He was still tempted to mention Falconer, and annoyed at his own indecision.

"Then I mustn't keep you," Scott-Marie said. They both stood up and went toward the door, and as they entered the passage the telephone bell rang in the room behind them.

"You answer it, sir, I can let myself out," Gideon said.

Scott-Marie hesitated, then turned back toward the remorseless insistence of the bell's ringing. "All right, do that - good night."

"Good night, sir." Gideon opened the door and noticed with wry amusement that the Commissioner of Police had the most elementary system of burglar prevention. He felt the rain wafting gently into his face and hesitated; he would get soaked if he were out long in this, but the call for Scott-Marie had prevented him from sending for a car. He would manage. He closed the door firmly. There was a police call box not far away, and he could wait on a nearby porch. Then a taxi came splashing past, its sign alight, and he let out a bellow which made the driver slam on his brakes. Sprinting after it, he was halfway between porch and taxi when he heard Scott-Marie behind him, with a parade-ground roar: *"Gideon! Gideon!"*

Gideon managed to pull himself up and half turned. "Coming, sir." He looked at the driver, a little man with a huge nose. "Wait for me, please."

He turned back to Scott-Marie, who was outlined against the light of the hall.

"Sir Richard Falconer is on the line," he called. "You'd better hear what he has to say."

17: Urgent Call

Scott-Marie turned back in to the house; Gideon hesitated and, rain making a film over his face and beading his eyebrows and hair, went to the taxi driver, who had pulled in and switched off his "For Hire" sign.

"Sorry," Gideon said, and put six shillings into his hand. "It might be too long a wait."

"No hurry where I'm concerned, Mr. Gideon," the driver said.

"Oh. Recognized, am I?"

"Yes, sir, often see you about. Be a privilege to take you as a passenger."

Gideon half smiled. "Thanks. I'll be as quick as I can." He went into the house and took out his handkerchief to dab his face dry. Every now and again, his habit of going without hat and coat let him down, and it was surprising how wet he had got in the past few minutes.

Scott-Marie was holding the receiver to his ear; once or twice he attempted to speak, but Falconer obviously talked him down. When he saw Gideon, he pointed, stabbing his finger toward the back of the house, and it dawned on Gideon that he was telling him to go somewhere—ah! The cloakroom, beneath the stairs. Gideon went in, dabbed himself with a towel, and came out feeling much drier. He found the Commissioner standing in the library doorway.

"Falconer is worried about his daughter, who has been missing for several hours," Scott-Marie announced, with a dry, almost wintry smile. "Naturally, he would like the whole of our resources concentrated on finding her. If we don't exert ourselves, he will undoubtedly bring all kinds of pressure to bear tomorrow, which could make unnecessary difficulties, but—" He spread his hands. "I do, of course, leave it to you."

As Gideon listened, he knew that he could no longer put off telling the Commissioner the whole story, and he wondered with sudden raw urgency whether Thwaites had discovered something more about the rumour of Falconer's involvement. He must find out as soon as possible; but first he had to tell Scott-Marie.

Falconer put down the receiver after talking to Scott-Marie and drew a hand across his head. He was trembling. His wife was astonished and, in a way, touched. He went across to a table, took a cigar from a silver box, pierced the end, then came back to the big couch and stood looking down on her.

"What did he say?" she asked.

"He told me that he would start inquiries at once, but—" Falconer paused to strike a match and to puff at the cigar. "But he pointed out that Christine can hardly be regarded as missing."

Gently, Charlotte Falconer said: "It isn't much after eleven o'clock, Richard."

"Do you mean that *you* don't regard her as missing?"

"I think she may simply have carried her rebellion a step further," Charlotte replied; for her to challenge his opinion so positively was almost daring.

"I do not believe that Christine would act so much out of character," Falconer insisted. "And if there is no news of her by morning—"

"Oh, there will be! She'll be back tonight."

"I hope so," Falconer said. "I hope so very much."

He broke off as Davies came in, soft-footed. Davies would only appear at this hour if there was an emergency or an unexpectedly late caller, and Falconer swung round on him with unusual vehemence.

"What is it?"

"A young man is here, sir," Davies said.

"Young man?"

"Perhaps it is Lancelot Judd," Charlotte said, getting up quickly.

"No, my lady, I would recognize Mr. Judd's voice," said Davies. "He has phoned here for Miss Christine several times. This gentleman did not give his name but said he has a message from Miss Christine. That is why I let him in."

"Where is he?" Falconer demanded.

"In the morning room," Davies answered.

"Tell him I'll see him very soon," Falconer said. "Where is Mr. Oliphant?"

"He went out earlier in the evening, sir, and told me that he might be late - might not be here until tomorrow, in fact."

Falconer nodded, and the butler went out, as soft footed as when he had entered. Falconer drew deeply at his cigar, where half an inch of greyish-white ash now showed, and began to move about nervously.

"I should have told Oily to stay in tonight" he said vexed: "This is no time for him to dally with his girlfriend." He paused, then blurted out: "Charlotte, I am deeply troubled about Christine. Have you the slightest reason to think that she might have eloped with this man Judd? Could this be the caller's message?"

"Good gracious!" exclaimed Charlotte. "The thought didn't cross my mind."

"You are not—you are not deliberately protecting her? Giving her time to get out of my reach?"

"No, Richard, I am not," answered Charlotte Falconer. She got up and moved toward him, took his hands in hers, and felt the chill of his fingers and the agitation which made him quiver as if an electric current were passing through his body. "No, my dear, I would not dream of doing such a thing to you. You can trust me, Richard, you can trust me absolutely."

He gripped her hands tightly for a few seconds, then let them go.

"I should know better than to doubt you" he said. "Well, I must go and see what this fellow has to say." He turned and hurried out, without looking backward, so he did not see how motionless his wife stood as she watched him. She was like a statue. He went into the hall, told Davies to stay within call, then turned in to the morning room. It was here that the family received casual guests whom they did not want to entertain officially.

A young man stood with his back to the fireplace; a tall young man dressed rather as an exquisite, with over-long hair beautifully groomed and shining golden in the soft light. His eyes, narrowed, were very bright. He wore a suede suit with unusually short lapels, and a carefully arranged cravat, and he looked very young, certainly no more than twenty-two or three. Christine's age. Falconer was tempted to demand "What do you know about Christine," but he fought for self-control

"Good evening."

"Good evening, Sir Richard. It is very good of you to see me."

It was a pleasing voice, which was one good thing, thought Falconer. But why didn't the youth come straight out with the message from Christine?

"I would not have called so late had it not been on an urgent matter." There was a hint of insolence in the youth's manner as he spoke.

"Be good enough to come to the point," Falconer said.

The young man did not answer, and belatedly it occurred to Falconer that he should have asked his name. He was in the grip of a tension such as he had not experienced for many years, but if he lost his control this apparently foppish young man could too easily take advantage of him. So he waited.

The stranger spoke with great precision.

"It concerns the safety of your daughter Christine, sir."

Falconer almost cried out: *"Safety?"* but he still maintained that iron self-control.

"Go on, please."

"Christine is late home tonight," the youth stated.

"I am aware of it."

"Aren't you curious about the reason?"

"I am always curious about the mental processes of the young."

"Are you, indeed," the young man said. "I said that my business concerns Christine's safety."

"I heard you."

"Aren't you concerned?"

"I am very concerned."

"I am glad to hear it," the young man said. "She can be returned to you, unharmed."

"If she isn't, then those responsible for harming her will rue it very much indeed," Falconer said grimly.

"I doubt that," said the young man. There was something almost feline in his manner, and now he gave the impression that he was fully aware that Falconer was hiding his fears and his tension, was suffering anguish; and that he, the youth, enjoyed what he was doing with sadistic relish. "I doubt *that* very much indeed. Don't you want to know where she is?"

"I want her here, unharmed."

"On certain terms," the young man said, "you may have exactly that."

"We can discuss terms afterward."

"Oh, no, Sir Richard. We shall discuss terms now."

"Tell me how much money you require in exchange for my daughter," Falconer said coldly. "I will consider the exchange then."

The young man smiled. He had a honey-brown complexion and his teeth were white and even. There was tawniness about his eyes, and his lips were well-shaped and soft.

"It is not a question of money," he stated.

"That I do *not* believe." Falconer took the stub of the cigar from his lips and laid it on an ashtray without shifting his gaze.

But it was difficult to keep his hand steady, difficult to prevent his voice from rising, and even more difficult to restrain the impulse to knock the smile off the sneering face in front of him.

"Whether you believe it or not, it's the truth," the young man insisted. "You have a remarkably fine collection of pictures and *objets d'art,* Sir Richard."

"We are not discussing my collection."

"I am," said the young man. "Perhaps I should introduce myself. My name is Robin Kell. I am reasonably intelligent, and I have a fair knowledge of art, especially paintings and small antiques. I am what you would doubtless call unscrupulous, possibly ruthless, and I do not hold human life in great esteem. We are born, we live, we die. Few of us make a very great impact. If you were to die, very few would miss you and several people would probably be glad to see you go. If your daughter were to die—" Robin Kell paused, and his manner was taunting, as if he wanted to make Falconer lose his self-control. But Falconer held on, finding it easier now, and the young man continued - "you might miss her for a while, and no doubt so would her mother. But who else would really care, Sir Richard? How much sense would her dying make to the world?"

There was a beading of sweat on Falconer's forehead and upper lip. "Go on," he said icily.

"Ah, yes. I was discussing your collection," said Robin Kell. "Has it all been honestly come by?"

Very deliberately, Falconer said: "Every item has been bought at a reasonable value, yes. Mr. Kell, unless you make arrangements to bring my daughter back here at once I shall send for the police."

"Oh, you would be most ill-advised," answered Robin softly. "If the police are told, you will certainly never see your daughter again. And you would lose not only Christine," he went on "but a unique chance to expand your collection at a remarkable rate and really very reasonably. I need no telling that paint and canvas mean more than flesh and blood to you - so let us have no talk of the police, Sir Richard."

Davies heard all of this, and also knew that, less than an hour before, Sir Richard had talked to Scott-Marie, demanding that the police give absolute priority to finding Christine. The certain thing now was that he, Davies, must do nothing unless Sir Richard told him to.

He himself was much more composed than he had been, Falconer realized with relief. In spite of his inner tensions, he could control his expression, and he did not believe that this young man had the slightest idea how the last words had slashed through him. He moved, and sat on the arm of a couch, crossing one leg over the other, and exerting every fibre of his being to appear calm and unconcerned.

"Mr. Kell," he said, "you can neither blackmail me nor bribe me. If you fail to make immediate arrangements to return my daughter, unharmed in any way, I shall telephone the police." He paused long enough to see a flicker of doubt in Robin Kell's eyes, and went on: "I am prepared to discuss a ransom. I am not prepared to allow delay. How much do you want?"

Robin did not answer but for the first time turned away, unfastened his jacket and trouser waistband, and drew out a linen-wrapped package, thin, and curled slightly to the shape of his body. He held the package in one hand as he refastened his waistband, and proffered it to Falconer.

"Your daughter and that for a hundred thousand pounds," he said. "It is a very good bargain."

Falconer handled the package, and knew that it was a picture but at that moment did not suspect which one. He felt a strange conflict within him: a desire to fling it into the youth's face and to order him to fetch Christine if he did not want the police here at once; and a desire to see what painting this was. It was a conflict he had known to some degree all his life. He was aware that a great number of people thought he was interested in the precious things he owned because of their value or because of their rarity; that his possessions were for possession's sake. But it was much more than that. Beauty, especially beauty created by man, had an effect on him that was like a slow-burning fire which sometimes burst into flame. He had first been scorched by this when, as a child, he had stood in rapt wonder in front of pictures in the National Gallery. It was more than desire, even though he desired to possess them as, from time to time, he desired a woman of rare beauty; and it was more than passion.

He loved them.

The artist, through his creation, stretched out and touched him, and it was like being hypnotized. He could not resist things of such beauty. In his youth he had read all he could about them. No matter what it was, painting or sculpture, jewel or piece of furniture, he felt a physical response. It was not simply the pleasure of floating because the beautiful things in this house were his, it was a fact that he knew sensuous pleasure at both the touch and the sight of them.

And now he felt sure that there was something in this package which the youth knew he would desire.

But he was also a man of integrity.

What the youth could not possibly understand, what no one could ever understand, was how deeply, how cruelly, he was torn; torn between his knowledge of what he *ought* to do, his desperate fears for Christine, and his compulsion to open this packet.

Then, in a flash of understanding that was like a revelation, he understood what he held in his hands.

18: The Ultimatum

Very slowly, Falconer went to a table, put the packet on it, untied the knot, and then took away the string. The linen itself was stuck down but he was able to pull it away. He saw the white wrapping paper underneath, secured with tape, and tried to ease it up with his thumbnail. His heart was thumping with almost frenzied beat. He knew that the colour had been drawn from his face, that his tension must be obvious if he looked up. The white paper tore with the sticky tape, and he pushed it aside.

Here was the canvas back of a picture.

Slowly, he turned it over. A sheet of thin sponge rubber, protecting the picture itself, dropped away as he looked down. The first glimpse told him how right he was; and also did much more. It seemed to tear at his heart, as if the hands, as if that withered thumb, broke out of the canvas and clutched at him through his very flesh and bones. As he straightened it and saw the whole picture for the first time, his breathing seemed to stop.

After a while, forcing himself back to normality, he became acutely aware of the youth staring at him. The time had come when he must look up.

Laying the painting on the couch as if indifferently, he yet contrived to place it so that he could still, when looking that way, feast his eyes upon its beauty. Wrenching his gaze away, he turned to Robin Kell.

"So you are the thief?" he asked.

"I am the thief."

"It is like having a price on your head."

"Yes," said Robin softly. "That is exactly what it is like."

"On no conditions will I take this picture."

"It is very beautiful," remarked Robin.

"I know how beautiful it is," replied Falconer stiffly. "But it is owned by the State. It is part of the national heritage."

"Don't give me that nonsense and don't fool yourself," replied Robin. "If it's anyone's national heritage, it is Spain's, and Britain plundered it." He drew in a deep breath. "It is superbly beautiful."

"It can never be part of a deal with you over my daughter," said Falconer.

"If it isn't, there will be no deal over Christine," retorted Kell.

"Tell me how much—"

"I want one hundred thousand pounds for the painting *and* Christine together," insisted Robin very softly. "If you don't pay, then I shall destroy the painting and you will have destroyed your daughter."

"But you can't destroy this!" cried Falconer, and his voice rang about the room and into the hall and up the stairs.

Davies stood absolutely still, appalled.

The cry reached the ears of Falconer's wife, who was at the head of the stairs, wondering whether to go down. She was startled by the passion in his voice, the emotion he had not shown for so long. She heard another voice but was unable to distinguish the words. As Christine had, much earlier, she stayed where she was, knowing that she must not disturb Richard and yet desperately anxious to know what was going on in that room.

Robin Kell stood unmoving but not unmoved, his smile broader than it had been since he had entered the room, giving the impression that he was on the verge of triumph. Falconer stared at him helplessly, shaken by his own outburst, by his uncontrollable anguish, by his feeling of despair caused as much by his fear of the destruction of this picture as by the loss of his daughter.

He knew - no one else could ever know, but *he* knew - which he most cared for, which he most longed to save.

Robin thought, He can't resist them both. He might have put up a fight against one or the other, but together they're irresistible. He did not look away from the man, and his smile deepened to raw gloating when Falconer's gaze turned, as if under a compulsion he could not resist, to look at the painting on the couch.

Falconer was aware of the near-hypnotic appeal of the painting, of the colours, of the face of the child prince. But his mind was gradually taking over from his emotions, and he was beginning to assess the situation objectively. His own great battle was still to come. This man was kidnapper, murderer, thief: and beyond reasonable doubt, a liar. He would take the hundred thousand pounds if he could get his hands on it, but there was no possible guarantee that he would give up the Velazquez or Christine. And even if the exchange could be guaranteed, what would be the right thing to do? Let this cold-blooded youth go, to prey upon others as he, Falconer, was being preyed upon, to kidnap their loved ones, using priceless treasures of men's making to satisfy his lust for money?

Whatever the result of his forthcoming struggle to decide, the more he could find out about this young man, the better; and he would find out more if he showed a convincing interest.

"So you think I can't destroy a piece of canvas with some paint daubed over it," said Kell. "It won't take long to prove I can, and I haven't time to waste." He moved his right hand toward his waist slowly. His trousers were low cut, with pockets slantwise toward the hips, and very closefitting. Suddenly he dipped into a pocket with incredible speed, and there was a click, a flash, and in the youth's right hand was a knife with a thin, glistening blade. He held this between his thumb and fingers, thumb uppermost. "How about a few slashes with this,

Sir Richard? Across the picture - and your daughter's face."

Falconer's breath hissed inward. "Don't!"

"I don't share your sensitivity," Kell jeered. "That is paint on canvas which represents money. I have a lot of things which represent money. And as for your daughter—well, she is a pretty girl, but pretty girls come by the dozen, so you can't influence me by sentiment any more than you can appeal to my conscience." He gave another of his slight, meaningful pauses, then went on: "You need to know who you're dealing with, don't you?"

"Yes," Falconer said. He clenched his fists until his knuckles showed white and the fingernails cut into the palms of his hands. Whatever happened, he told himself, he must keep calm; must appear to be unmoved by anything this young savage said. Only by keeping calm could he even hope to gain the upper hand. "What do you mean, you have a lot of things which represent money?" he asked, forcing his voice to remain steady.

"I mean I am one of the best art thieves in the business, and I've been busy for a long time."

"You have—more such pictures as this?" Falconer asked hoarsely. How could he possibly think of allowing this man to stay free, yet if he didn't cooperate with him, what would happen to the Velazquez? And what - Falconer felt himself growing pale - what in heaven's name would happen to his daughter?

Kell nodded.

"Many, many more and I'm sure you wouldn't like to see them destroyed, would you, Sir Richard? But they will be - and that pretty daughter of yours as well - if you don't do as I say."

"How do I know you're telling the truth?"

"You know I'm telling the truth about "The Prince," don't you?"

"I should want much more evidence."

"You'll get your evidence every time we do a deal," Kell said coldly. "We've talked long enough, Falconer. Do you want "The

Prince" and do you want your daughter? You can have both for one hundred thousand pounds in deposits at different banks in different countries. As proof of my good faith I'll leave you "The Prince," and as proof of yours I've got your daughter."

"I will not gamble with—" Falconer began.

"You're not gambling," Kell interrupted. "You don't have any chance unless you accept my terms." He gave a little laugh, not altogether gloating, at least partly because he was so pleased with himself. "Keep away from the police," he warned again. "Don't forget that calling them in would be absolutely fatal. I'll be in touch with you tomorrow to arrange details." He paused for a long time, and then said, "Do you mind if I let myself out?"

He pressed the knife, and the blade snapped back inside the handle. Putting it back into his pocket, he moved toward Falconer and the door. Falconer stood still, as if deliberately blocking his path, then moved aside very slowly. Kell walked across the main hall to the front door, looking up the stairs and along the passages but seeing no one. Falconer moved but did not go to the front door, which Kell opened easily. Kell stepped outside and closed the door behind him.

Davies appeared from a doorway, but Falconer motioned him away.

As he disappeared, Falconer looked up and saw Charlotte, now at the head of the stairs, and although she was so far away, her anxiety came clearly through to him, both in her expression and in the stiffness of her movements. In turn, she saw a tension in him that seemed almost to distort his face, a tension that seemed to have aged him ten years in the past half hour. He moved toward her, and as he went up the stairs his eyes seemed to burn. She stood still, holding her hands out toward him, half in comfort, half in fear.

"Is she—is she all right?"

"Yes," Falconer said, in a grating voice. "So far, she is." He took his wife's hands, gripping them tightly. "Charlotte," he went on, "I have a great deal to think about, and—I don't want to be alone tonight." He broke off, and the muscles of his throat moved as if he were trying to speak but could not.

She closed her eyes and seemed to sway, but after a few moments she steadied again, and said quietly: "Then why don't you come up to me?"

Falconer went downstairs, wrapped the painting and took it up to his own room, rolling it loosely before placing it in a capacious wall safe. Then he went to his dressing table and picked up a photograph of Christine and stood looking at it for a long time. At last he put it back, drank a little brandy, then ran a bath. At half past twelve, he went to his wife's room.

Robin Kell went out of Falconer House into the soft penetrating rain of the October night. All the street lamps had haloes; so did the headlamps of the few cars he passed. He looked along the sides of the house and at the doorways of the houses opposite, but saw no sign of anyone watching. To make doubly certain, he walked past the rows of parked cars toward Piccadilly, then, when he reached the end of the street, turned back and walked in the other direction. But he saw no one, no sign of movement in the parked cars. Satisfied now that he was not being watched, he turned another corner and got into his red Morris 1100. Once in, he waited for a few moments to reassure himself still further that he had not been followed, and even when he switched on the lights and drove off, he watched his driving mirror very closely.

By the time he reached Hampstead, he felt not only secure but exultant.

A plainclothes policeman in a front room of an empty house nearly opposite Falconer's switched on his walkie-talkie and reported to Information at Scotland Yard: "Kell left Falconer's without the package."

A uniformed policeman trying the front doors of some shops in Park Lane switched on his walkie-talkie and reported, also to Information: "Kell drove north through Hyde Park, moving at moderate speed."

And information, keeping close track, took in report after report:

"Kell is heading east along Oxford Street."
"Kell has turned left past Selfridge's Food Department."
"Kell is passing Lord's Cricket Ground and heading north."
"Kell is at Swiss Cottage."
"Kell is heading up the hill toward the pond."
"Kell is in Hampstead Village."
"Kell has parked in the High Street. He is locking his car."

All these reports were passed through on the teletype machine; the strips were cut out and pasted up, and sent to Thwaites, who was alone in an office which he shared during the day with four other Chief Inspectors. He was a little on edge, not because he was tired but because since speaking to Gideon on the telephone he, had begun to regret having done so. He would never have interrupted Gideon normally, and the truth was that three double whiskies on an empty stomach had given him Dutch courage. This had evaporated almost immediately when the Superintendent in charge at Wembley had called him.

"Would you like to know where my chaps dropped Gee-Gee, Harold?" he said.

"Yes - where?" Thwaites had asked eagerly.

"The home of the great man himself."

"But he *is* the great man."

"Not to Sir Reginald Scott-Marie, he isn't."

"My God," Thwaites had breathed. "The Commissioner."

"Himself," the Wembley man had confirmed. "But don't worry too much; you're not far off retirement, are you?"

Thwaites had managed to echo the other's laughter, but it was a very hollow echo. He had almost *told* Gideon he ought to come here, to the Yard, and not waste his time by going home.

God! And Gideon would be coming here straight from Scott-Marie. Thwaites, checking over everything he had done and all the reports that had come in during the evening, munched a sandwich and drank more black coffee than he really needed. At all costs, he must be at his most effective when Gideon arrived.

Thwaites's interoffice telephone rang, probably with another report.

"Thwaites here," he said.

"Gee-Gee's just arrived," a man told him urgently.

"Oh! Thanks."

The other rang off, and Thwaites never learned who it was. He brushed his lips, pushed the tray aside, dusted some crumbs off his jacket, and then studied the summary of the reports. He had them off verbatim when his telephone rang again.

"Thwaites," he said, heart beating fast.

"I'm in my office," Gideon stated, and rang off.

Thwaites put down the receiver slowly and stood up. He had not felt like this in years, and could not remember feeling like it with Gideon before. He could not understand himself, did not realize it was because he knew he had stepped out of line and had no experience of Gideon's likely reaction, but he did know that Gideon had sounded pretty abrupt.

Within a minute of the call, he tapped on Gideon's door. As he waited, he was acutely aware of the stillness and the quiet, characteristic of the Yard at night and particularly noticeable after the bustle of the day. He could hear Gideon talking and wondered who else was with him. A possibility sprang to his mind and went through him like a knife. Not *Scott-Marie?*

"Come in," Gideon called at last, and Thwaites squared his shoulders and opened the door.

Gideon was sitting behind his desk and no one else was in the room. Gideon waved to a chair, made a note on a pad, and then settled back and said, in the most amiable of voices: "Sit down, Harold. If you're the same as I am these days, late nights make you leg-weary."

"Er—" Thwaites dropped into a chair, covered with confusion of his own making. "I know *exactly* what you mean, sir." Now he had the sense to leave Gideon to set the ball rolling, and was already feeling very much more himself.

Gideon bent down, took out his whisky and two glasses, and looked up.

"What do you like with yours?"

"If you don't mind, sir, I'll give it a miss," Thwaites said. "That's if you don't mind, sir."

"I'll give it a miss, too," said Gideon. "Well, what makes you think de Courvier is number three in the Velazquez killings?"

"I've compared a photograph of the knife or dagger wound with the one on Slater's body - Brighton sent pictures up. I've had Mr. Thompson look at them, and we both agree that it looks very much like the same kind of wound. And de Courvier is an old associate of Jenkins and Slater. We've established that." He went on very slowly: "But the thing that's rather shaken me, sir, is a report that Christine Falconer, Sir Richard's daughter, was seen to go into Judd's shop this morning. Division sent a car to look at the place, and the driver recognized her - her photograph is often in the papers. I've a nasty feeling that the shop ought to have been watched all the time."

"Wasn't it?" Gideon asked sharply.

"No, sir, not until tonight, and that's my fault. But it is being watched now, and—well, perhaps the best thing is to show you the reports as they came in." He pushed the sheet of teletype messages across Gideon's desk, and then added: "The man known as Kell is back there now, sir - in Judd's shop, I mean. It's remarkable, isn't it, that he spent well over half an hour in Falconer's house at this time of night? And he had a biggish flat package when he went in, but not when he came out. He was seen concealing it under his jacket on the porch, but his movements were too free for it to have been there when he left. It is remarkable, sir, isn't it?"

19: The Dilemma

Yes, thought Gideon, it was very remarkable indeed. Fresh in his mind was Falconer's approach to Scott-Marie. Would a man with anything on his conscience make such an approach to the Commissioner? On the face of it, it didn't make sense. He pondered as he looked at the pasted messages, then looked up, frowning.

"What package do you say Kell had with him when he went to Falconer House?"

"It was about the size of an open newspaper, and he seemed to wrap it round himself," Thwaites said. "It could easily have been a canvas."

"So that's what's in your mind," Gideon said, heavily. "It could have been the Velazquez."

"And it is perhaps now in Sir Richard Falconer's possession, sir."

"Yes," agreed Gideon. "So it appears. Let's have the whole story again."

"Very well, sir. Kell's a friend of Lancelot Judd, who owns the Hampstead shop. He was seen going to Falconer House carrying the packet, this evening. He went in with the packet but apparently did not bring it away. That was the time I decided to have him trailed very closely, sir. He went back to the shop about eleven o'clock and is still there. And he had nothing with him, as far as I know. If it was a canvas, it's probably still in Falconer House."

Gideon grunted.

"So we ought to search."

Thwaites drew his breath rather uneasily through his full lips, and after a few seconds, said: "I would certainly apply for a warrant if it were anyone else, sir, but I would hate to go wrong on this one."

"Yes," said Gideon. "So would I. Is Falconer House still being watched?"

"Closely, sir."

"Any instructions given?"

"To follow anyone who leaves," answered Thwaites. "I didn't feel I could go any further on my own authority, sir. It's been worrying me all the evening. I tried to get Mr. Hobbs but he wasn't home; he's visiting a sister and travelling back by road so I couldn't get him. And when I learned that the man de Courvier was dead I called you."

"Quite right," said Gideon. "Go down to Information, will you, and tell them to stop anyone going in or out of Falconer House. I don't care who it is: Sir Richard himself or anyone. They can go anywhere provided you make sure they haven't got that painting. All clear?"

"Yes, sir." Thwaites, obviously lighter-hearted than for some time, almost bounced toward the door.

"Thwaites!"

"Sir?"

"You did say that girl was not seen to leave, didn't you?"

"I did, sir," said Thwaites

"And the Hampstead shop is now being closely watched?"

"By half a dozen men, sir."

"Have anyone who leaves that shop stopped and searched, too," ordered Gideon.

"I *will*, sir!"

Thwaites let the door swing to, and it banged slightly.

Gideon glanced at it absently. His forehead was wrinkled in a deep frown. With Hobbs not available and most of the senior superintendents difficult to get at during a weekend, he would have to take this job over himself. He knew that he should, and he wanted to; an issue as delicate as this should not be left to others.

His chief concern now was for the missing girl.

Christine lay on a mattress in a corner of the back room, her legs and hands tied, a scarf bound round her mouth. She had a throbbing headache and her eyes were so heavy she could no longer keep them open. She did not know how long she had been tied up but she did know that Lance had been on the premises alone for a long time and had left her here. *Lance,* to do such a thing! *Lance,* whom she had so loved, with whom there had been such deep pleasure in this place only a few hours ago. He seemed to be so desperately afraid of Robin Kell that after a few half-hearted protests, he did whatever the other man told him.

She heard movements, but she could not see.

She heard someone close by, and knew that Lance had pushed aside the curtain. Light flooded the little alcove, bright enough to hurt her eyes. She did not open them and resolutely faced the wall.

"Chris," Lance whispered.

She pretended that she had not heard.

"Chris, it will be all right, I promise you."

Did he lie even to himself? She wondered helplessly.

He touched her shoulder, and it was like being touched by fingers of ice.

"Chris, do you want anything?"

She could not answer because the scarf was tied so tightly. He knew that and yet he could bring himself to ask such a question. She did not stir. She was half bemused, anyhow; the effect of whatever drug they had given her had not really worn off.

"Chris," he said again, his voice so close that she could feel his warm breath on her ear and on her cheek, "he's gone to see your father. Your father won't let you down."

At last she turned to look at him. There was nothing she

could say because of the gag, but she could face facts. Here was the man she loved and who had declared his love with such fierce passion, looking at her and doing nothing - *nothing* to help.

"Robin will come to terms with him," he insisted.

At that, she closed her eyes, in weariness and with disgust.

"I tell you he will! Robin knows what he's doing and he'll make arrangements with your father. I'm absolutely certain."

Christine could believe that he meant it; he was telling her that Robin had gone to collect a ransom for her and that her father would pay. How much would it be? A big sum, that was certain. Ten thousand pounds? Oh, she was worth more than that even to her father. He would not miss such a sum, would think nothing of paying it for a picture or a casket. He would buy her freedom as he would buy a work of art, and afterward would make her feel that she owed him even more, would expect her to be his prisoner for as long as he desired.

And yet—

He *had* warned her against Lance.

But he had warned her against every friend not of his own choosing.

"And I—I won't let Robin harm you," Lance was saying, as if he believed his empty words. "I promise you, I—What was that?"

There had been a sound downstairs, and it was followed by another, unmistakably the front door of the shop. Lance sprang up and pulled the curtains so that she could see nothing, then bounded toward the staircase.

"Robin! Is that you?"

"Who do you think it is?" Robin demanded. He came running up the stairs, very light of foot. "It's working out perfectly. I've touched on Falconer's besetting weakness." He spoke with absolute conviction. "He's in love with art and its treasures! They're his idols and his mistresses rolled into one. If he had to choose between the Velazquez and his darling Christine, he'd ditch Christine. Oh, boy, are we on to a good thing!"

Christine felt as if a great weight had suddenly dropped on her, and her heart beat in dull, sickening throbs.

20: The Plot

Lancelot Judd watched as Robin began to dance and pirouette, light on his feet as a ballet dancer. Swinging to a halt, he gave a burst of excited laughter.

"Who wants to be a millionaire?" Robin hummed the tune, and began to pirouette again, then stopped immediately in front of Lance. "And *you're* on a bed of roses, Sir Lancelot, you'll be the millionaire's son-in-law! Which reminds me, how is our stricken fawn?"

"She—she's still sleeping. You—you won't do anything to hurt her, will you?"

"My dear Sir Lancelot, what makes you think I could be so ungallant? Would I harm your wife-to-be - especially as, married to you, she will be able to bring all the necessary psychological pressures on the great Sir Richard. Do as we say dear Daddy-in-law, or think what we'll do to your daughter." He laughed again. "Do you know, he didn't offer me a drink. But you will, won't you?"

Lance turned to a small oak chest on which stood bottles and glasses.

"What will you have?" he asked eagerly.

"Champagne, Sir Lancelot, what else will suit the mood of the night? Champagne! All right, I'll settle for a whisky-and-soda!" Now he moved about the room, rhythmic and self-assured despite his excitement. "The superb thing is that everything is working exactly according to plan. I'll even be able to send for Marie; she was so edgy after the sad death of

Jenkins and Slater that I thought she ought to rest." He sat down in a large armchair and stretched his legs out in front of him, took the glass which Lance proffered, and said "Cheers!" and drank. "Now to business! Falconer has the Velazquez and it nearly gave him a fit, he was so excited. Tomorrow he will pay me for it, and then I'll show him some photographs of other treasures - treasures he'd sell his wife, his daughter, and his soul for. You will go and see him and if you can marry Christine, and very soon you'll be one of the family. From that time on, I will sell him treasures as he requires them. The only problem will be a place to keep them, but I expect Sir Richard will look after that. There must be very large cellars and vaults at Falconer House." He drank again and looked up at his friend, eyes aglow. "Can *you* see where it can possibly go wrong?"

"Not—er—not really," Lance said. "Except—er—after this will Christine *want* to marry me?"

"For her father's, mother's, and honour's sake, she will marry you," said Robin positively.

No, no, no! Christine cried within herself. Not now, not after this. Never.

But she caught her breath as she heard Robin go on.

"She is in love with you, Sir Lancelot. Although for some strange, pathological reason, I am proof against usual human emotions, needing only sex shared with enthusiasm, I can still see the unmistakable evidence of these emotions in others. And Christine is the type of woman who would stay faithful to a man no matter how he beat or ill-treated her, no matter how many other women he flaunted before her distressed gaze. She's a natural masochist. Look how she suffers the dictates of dear Daddy, pretending to resent them but always going back for more. Oh, she'll marry you, (a) because she's in love with you, (b) because it will keep her father out of trouble, and (c) because if she refused and really meant it then I'd cut her pretty throat!"

"Don't say that!" cried Lancelot.

"Think what incentive you have to be a truly great lover,"

Robin said. "Go to her now. Wake her with your prowess and woo her with your love. You *are* in love with her, aren't you?"

"God knows I am," muttered Lancelot Judd. "God knows I am."

As she heard that, Christine's despair lifted a little, and although she told herself that it was madness, that they could never marry, she could never be happy in such a marriage, she was aware in her whole body of the gentle touch of his hands.

"It will be all right," he whispered. "I always said it would be all right."

She felt sure that he actually believed it. In his way, he must be the most naive man in the world.

For a long time, while all these things were going on, Richard Falconer lay by his wife's side. He had known, as she had known, a few moments of diffidence not far removed from shyness, but these had soon passed. Their shared warmth was comfort, and for a while he lay wide awake, his muscles tense and aching slightly, his head taut with physical as well as emotional strain, his heart leaden. After a while, he turned on his side and put his arm round her, feeling her body respond to his.

"Are you awake?" he whispered, knowing well that she was.

"Yes," she said. "Wide awake."

"I don't know what to do," he said. "I really don't know what to do. I am afraid. I really am afraid that Christine is in grave danger."

"What *can* we do?" asked Charlotte.

She sensed that she must lie there, unmoving yet showing her awareness of him, that she must not show signs of agitation or distress, because it might drive him away again, to the distant places where he had been over a long and weary time. So, she stilled her own deep fears and asked him, simply, what they could do.

"That young man who came here," he said, "is a friend of Lancelot Judd. . . . And he is—*evil,* Charlotte. Evil is the only word to describe him. A thief, too, and no fool." He stopped but she waited without prompting, and he went on: "He left the stolen Velazquez with me."

This time, she started, her body stiffening, and half turned her head.

"'The Prince'?"

"Yes," Falconer answered. "The picture itself, not a copy - I have no doubt at all. I've put it in my safe."

"But—" she began, twisting her head round still further. Then, acutely aware of his need, she forced herself to appear relaxed. "You can't keep it, surely?" she asked gently.

"No. No, I can't possibly keep it. Although the temptation is—" He paused, and she felt his fingers pressing into her, powerful but free of passion. "The temptation is awful, Charlotte. I—I *love* these treasures. I *love* them."

"I know," she said, and, in a whisper that he could hardly hear, went on: "Each like a beautiful woman. It is a long time since I stopped being jealous of them."

"Jealous?" he echoed wonderingly, and after a pause he asked, "He offered me that and many more, and threatened, if I refused to buy, both to destroy them and to kill Christine. Do you see how fiendishly clever that is? To offer me what I crave for a sum of money which I can well afford, and Christine's safety to make my connivance seem justifiable. Charlotte, Charlotte," he went on, his voice almost breaking, "how *can* I cooperate with this man? How can I leave him free to steal more of the world's treasures, threatening, bullying, *killing* those who stand in his way? Yet if I *don't* cooperate, what will happen to the treasures he already has? And *what* will happen to Christine?"

As Charlotte turned to face him, her body astir with fear, he held her tightly as if they were as much part of each other as on the night when their daughter had been conceived, and he said in a voice more broken still: "It's a terrible dilemma, Charlotte. What *are* we to do?"

21: Decision

Yes, Charlotte thought bitterly, it is a terrible dilemma. She thought of Christine, and full awareness of the danger pierced through her for the first time; the true horror of it. That it should have taken such a situation to melt the ice which had for so long kept them apart was anguish in itself. But she must not show her feelings too much; if she gave way to them, she might undo what good had already come out of the situation. She had to fight for him, and for themselves, and for Christine.

"How did you leave the situation with this man?" she asked.

"He's to be in touch with me tomorrow"

"Are you *sure* Christine is safe until then?"

"He'll know that if she isn't kept unharmed, there can be no business between us."

"So *that's* her insurance."

"It's the only insurance we can have," Falconer told her. "I am quite sure that she is in no danger tonight. If I could rest for a few hours, I might see more clearly in the morning. Even if I rest only for an hour or two."

While he lay sleeping, Charlotte's mind was in a turmoil; one moment she was sure that they must tell the police at once, the next equally sure that at all costs they must protect Christine. After a while, she could not lie there any longer, and she eased herself away from Richard and then out of bed.

He did not stir.

She went into her dressing room and made some tea and

drank it while fighting the battle out with herself. For the first time since they had married, she was in a position to influence him on what course to take. Yet she had never wanted so much to leave the decision to him.

Gideon was still at his desk at half past twelve that Sunday night, and still undecided, but he was veering more and more toward postponing any decision until the morning. There was no certainty that Christine Falconer was in danger, and with the house and the shop closely watched, nothing could be brought away. A raid to search Falconer House now would be difficult to stage, difficult perhaps to justify. Yet if he asked Falconer to let the police search, then obviously the man would have a chance to hide anything he had illegally. Gideon did not want and did not mean to be swayed by Falconer's wealth and position, but if Thwaites was wrong and the search was abortive, the newspapers would make a tremendous fuss and the prestige of the Yard would be severely damaged. If ever there was a time to be sure before acting, this was it.

He drummed on his desk, going over every aspect of the case, measuring Thwaites's suspicions against the probabilities and tonight's evidence. He yawned suddenly. Probably the best thing *would* be to sleep on it. He could put his head down on a bed in one of the first aid cubicles, used for such a purpose. He had telephoned Kate when he arrived and told her he would probably not be home. She had been yawny and tired and very happy.

"Such a lovely evening, George."

And here *he* was, yawning and postponing a decision.

On that instant, he closed his mouth like a trap, pulled a telephone forward, and put in a call to Hampstead, the KL Division Headquarters.

"Any developments at Judd's shop?" he demanded.

"No, sir. I had a report in only three or four minutes ago. Everything's in darkness there."

"Thanks," grunted Gideon, and put down the receiver only to

lift it again and call the AB Division Headquarters, about Falconer House.

"No excitement," answered the Superintendent in charge. "I went out there myself and came back only twenty minutes ago. Everything's quiet. The last person seen to go in was Oliphant, Falconer's personal assistant, and he carried nothing in the way of a case or a parcel."

"The house is closely watched?"

"Tight as a drum, sir. Like Judd's shop."

"Good. I'm going over to Falconer's place myself, to talk to him," Gideon told him, hardly aware that he had come to such a positive decision. "I'll have a couple of men with me, but I want your chaps alerted."

"They will be! Like me along with you, sir?"

"Do you want to come?"

"Not particularly," answered the Superintendent. "There's been a bank robbery in Park Lane, and I ought to go there."

"Then do that," said Gideon. He put down the receiver and almost immediately picked it up again, dialled a third time, and said: "I want a car, driver, and one other man waiting for me in five minutes. Not a minute more. Do you know if Mr. Thwaites is still in the building?"

"He's having a kip - sleeping upstairs, sir."

Gideon grunted and rang off, took an old raincoat off a peg, and slipped it on as he went upstairs to the first aid room. Two men as well as Thwaites were there, heavily asleep, one of them snoring loudly. Thwaites himself looked very tired and old; he was sleeping in an undershirt, and one big, rather flabby arm was over a blanket. It seemed a pity to wake him, but if this was the kill, Thwaites had to be in on it. Gideon shook him slightly by the shoulder, and Thwaites was alert instantly, his eyes flickering.

"Be downstairs in five minutes," Gideon said. "We're going to Falconer House."

Before Gideon was out of the room, Thwaites was pushing the blanket back. Gideon went down to Information, told the night superintendent what he was going to do, and added: "If there's any word at all from West End or Hampstead, make certain I know at once."

"Be sure we will, sir."

Gideon went down the steep steps toward the courtyard, where his car was already waiting, the driver and another man standing by it. One opened the back door and Gideon got in, grunting with the effort. He was getting too big around the middle for bending double. He heard someone hurrying down the steps and guessed it was Thwaites.

"Mr. Thwaites will join me," he said. "Let him in at the other door."

Soon, Thwaites was crammed against him, breathing rather hard, looking very pale.

"Driver, I'm going to Falconer House, near Park Lane," Gideon said. "You two are to wait by the side of the car. The house is already being watched. Don't take any part in anything unless you get instructions from Mr. Thwaites or me. Understood?"

"All clear, sir."

Gideon turned to Thwaites, and went on speaking as if there had been no change of audience: "Nothing new has turned up but I'm not happy at waiting until the morning, and I know you're not. We'll go in together, but I'll see Falconer on my own. You join us only if I call you."

"I understand," Thwaites said, and then he added after a long pause: "I'm very glad you're having a go, sir."

"I hope we stay glad," Gideon said, and sat back as they drove through the still steadily falling rain. It was past two o'clock when the car pulled up outside Sir Richard Falconer's house, where a single light shone in the porch but none at any of the windows.

Falconer was aware of deep sleep, heavy sleep to which he was not accustomed, and then of his wife's voice and the pressure of her hand on his shoulder. He opened his eyes to a dim, not dazzling light, but even that was too bright for him. He saw his wife through his lashes, and remembered what had happened and where he was. Then, seeing the anxiety on her face, he suddenly thought: *Christine!* and struggled to a sitting position.

"What is it? What—"

"It's all right; it's not about Christine," Charlotte said. "There are two policemen downstairs, one of them is Commander Gideon. He insists on seeing you, Richard. I couldn't put him off until the morning."

Falconer hitched himself further back in the bed.

"What time is it?"

"Just after two."

"It could be news of Christine," he said tautly. "Gideon is the man whom Scott-Marie would assign to the inquiry." He pushed the bedclothes back, and she helped him into his dressing gown. "Who let them in?"

"Oily did."

"So he's back?"

"He hadn't gone to sleep, so he told Davies not to get out of bed," Charlotte said.

"Have him make some coffee, will you? Strong, with plenty of sugar."

"I'll see to it," she promised. "He's waiting outside."

Falconer tied the dressing-gown cord tightly about his waist as he went out of the room. Oliphant, a smoking jacket over pyjamas trousers, moved toward him from the head of the stairs.

"Richard, there is something I must tell you," he said.

"Not now, Oily, later—"

"Now. As the police are here, it is vital."

Falconer stood very still and made the other come toward him. Oliphant was obviously agitated, for once not knowing what to say. Downstairs in the hall, Gideon and Thwaites could just be seen, too far away to overhear, not too far to know that something was being said.

"What difference do the police make?" Falconer demanded impatiently.

"Richard, I—I should have told you long ago, but I—I didn't know it might matter. Two of the Monets and one of the Cellini caskets in the long gallery were" - Oliphant caught his breath - "they were stolen."

"*Stolen?*" Falconer echoed unbelievingly. "And you knew it?"

"Yes. I—I was offered them at very good prices, and—well, I fell for the temptation of making a profit." Oliphant sounded terribly distressed.

"And you not only bought them on my behalf knowing them to be stolen, but made a fat killing," Falconer said.

"I—I could explain it if—You see, I had personal problems, and the dealers—"

"We can go into this later," Falconer said, in a forbidding voice. "Now you fear that the police may have come here for these stolen pieces?"

"They—they have a search warrant," Oliphant muttered.

"I see. If they identify these works, I shall disclaim all knowledge of their being stolen. And in my case I shall require a full history of each purchase, the dealer involved, the money paid, and the commission you received." Falconer nodded dismissal.

He went downstairs, and as he did so the two men in the hallway turned: Gideon, massive and aggressive in the slightest movement, a man for whom Falconer had an instant respect, and Thwaites, for whom he felt nothing at all. He greeted them with a word and a gesture and led Gideon into the room where he had seen Robin Kell. If he felt any surprise that the other man did not follow them, he showed none. Brandy, glasses, and decanters were on a small table.

"Will you—" he began.

"No thank you, sir," said Gideon. "I am Commander Gideon of the Criminal Investigation Department of the Metropolitan Police and I would like some information from you, please."

"Have you traced my daughter?" demanded Falconer sharply.

"We think we know where she is, sir. We have no reason to believe that she went there against her will or is missing in the official sense of the word." Before Falconer could interrupt, before it was possible to judge the extent of his relief, Gideon went on in a flat, formal voice, "We have reason to believe that you have in your possession a painting, known as 'The Prince,' painted by the Spanish artist Velazquez, knowing it to be stolen. Is that true, sir?"

There was a long pause, during which Gideon sensed the truth yet realized there was something here which he did not understand. Then the silence was broken by the clink of cups and the rattle of spoons on a silver tray. Lady Falconer, not Oliphant, brought in coffee, and hesitated in the doorway. Falconer seemed oblivious, but Gideon was quick to notice the woman and said: "Your husband may prefer to be alone, ma'am."

"No," said Falconer quietly. "No. My wife knows about the situation. I told her earlier tonight, Commander. You are quite right. I have the painting. It was offered to me for a hundred thousand pounds. I was told that if I did not buy it, my daughter would be. killed. Did you give me to understand that you know where my daughter is?"

Charlotte moved to a small table, and very carefully placed the coffee tray in position. She turned to Gideon, her eyes pleading.

Very heavily but without any inflection in his voice, Gideon asked: "Was that before or after you telephoned Sir Reginald Scott-Marie, sir?"

"After," answered Falconer. "Some time afterward. I don't think I would have had the courage to talk to him had I know the danger that my daughter was in. He—"

"Who do you mean by 'he'?" interrupted Gideon.

"The man who offered me the painting, a young man named Robin Kell, or who called himself Robin Kell," answered

Falconer. "He warned me that if I consulted you, not only would he murder my daughter but he would destroy many Old Masters, paintings which he has stolen over a period of several years. And for what it is worth, I believe him capable of committing both crimes, Commander."

There was a long, tense silence before Thwaites said from the hall: "My God! That would be awful!"

22: The Murderer

Gideon was aware of the conflicting tensions of everyone present. Of Thwaites, who had come forward to watch Lady Falconer, just inside the room, his concern for the treasures that were in danger. Of Lady Falconer, so composed when she had come in, so shattered now. Of Falconer himself, standing there with a dignity he had shown from the moment he had come downstairs, very different from the man who had tried so hard to use his position to influence Scott-Marie.

"Do you know where the stolen goods are?" Gideon asked, as flatly as ever.

"I only know that Kell said he could produce them within the hour."

"He'll have them at Hampstead," interpolated Thwaites.

"That's quite possible," Gideon agreed. "But we need to be sure." He moved to ease the atmosphere, giving Lady Falconer a brief smile. "If a cup of coffee wouldn't be inconvenient, ma'am .... Come in, Thwaites.... Sir Richard, Chief Inspector Thwaites has been working on the Velazquez robbery and it was he who traced Robin Kell to a small antique shop in Hampstead.... Ah, thank you, ma'am.... No biscuits, thank you." He sipped coffee and then went on: "We have to be sure before we know exactly how best to search the shop.... Would you mind letting us have the painting, sir?" He actually smiled at Falconer. "I would like Thwaites's opinion on its authenticity."

"If Sir Richard identifies—" Thwaites began, and immediately subsided.

"I'll get it," said Falconer.

"Go with Sir Richard, Chief Inspector," Gideon ordered, without hinting that he was simply making sure that Falconer could make no attempt to escape. He drank more coffee as the two went out, and he was left alone with Lady Falconer. He had seen her occasionally at social and official functions, but had never realized how very lovely she was. At close quarters, anxiety stricken, she was superb. "I know how you must be feeling, my lady," he said. "At least it won't be long now."

She asked huskily, "Do you think this man Kell's threats are serious, Commander?"

What shall I tell her? Gideon wondered. He had no doubt at all that Kell was involved with the coldblooded murders of the three men who had helped him; nothing suggested that he had a soft spot in him, and once he knew that he was cornered, he might well kill and destroy out of sheer spite.

Before he could speak, Lady Falconer said, "I can see that you do believe the threats are serious."

"Yes," admitted Gideon. "I'm afraid they may be very serious indeed."

"Is there anything—anything I can possibly do?"

Gideon deliberated, then put down his coffee cup, an excuse to get a little nearer, and studied her intently.

"There is nothing at all except help your husband," he told her. "If Sir Richard will go to this Hampstead shop in the morning and demand to see the other stolen items before he makes a decision about what to do, then I think we have a chance."

"Is it so important that you know whether the art treasures are there?" Charlotte asked, a glint of scorn in her eyes.

"Very important indeed," answered Gideon. "If Kell has the stolen goods, he can use them to bargain with; if he hasn't, then I hate to say that the only bargaining will be over your daughter." He heard the others returning and glanced around, seeing the picture in Thwaites's hands and the radiance in the

North Countryman's eyes. "I was just explaining to Lady Falconer, sir, that if Kell has the other stolen goods you could agree to talking terms for buying them on condition that he releases your daughter. That way, I think you will have a very good chance. Once we get your daughter away from the shop, we can concentrate on getting our man. If he carried out his threat to destroy the art treasures—"

Gideon broke off, shrugging slightly, and watching both Falconer, the collector, and Thwaites, the man who could only worship things of such beauty from afar. They looked exactly the same: appalled and yet full of hope.

"I understand the situation," Falconer said, at last. "I am not sure that I understand the risk."

"The risk is that if Kell comes to suspect that you are working with us, he could kill both your daughter and you before we could save you," Gideon said. "The risk is as simple as that."

It seemed an age before Falconer said, "I will take it."

"Now," Gideon said as they left the house, "we want everything laid on before daylight, so that Kell can't suspect the shop is being watched. We need men on the roof across the street, men on the roof next door, who can swing into the windows of the flat. We want a fire engine with a turntable available nearby - no reason why it shouldn't have been called out earlier for an imaginary outbreak two or three shops along the street. The moment Falconer has gone into that shop, we want to be absolutely ready." He hardly paused before going on: "We'll need tear gas and our men must be masked. Everything will be a matter of split-second timing. Lay it all on, and let me have a report in detail first thing in the morning."

"Sir Richard," said Robin Kell, on the telephone at ten o'clock next morning.

"Yes," Falconer said.

"I hope you've made up your mind."

"I have given it a lot of thought," Falconer said. "And I will accept on one condition."

"You aren't in any position to make conditions."

"Nevertheless, I am making one," Falconer retorted coldly. "I want to know what the other goods are and I want to see them before I pay any money or give any undertakings. And I want a very quick decision, or I shall do what I should no doubt have done in the first place - go to the police."

"You bloody fool, if you do that I'll cut her throat!"

"What other consideration do you think would make me even contemplate doing business with you?" demanded Falconer, and rang off.

Gideon, sitting in his office, almost gritting his teeth because he so wanted to be at Hampstead, snatched up his telephone when it rang just after ten o'clock.

"Kell has telephoned me," Falconer said. "He didn't like my terms but I think he will agree."

"Sir Richard?" asked Robin Kell.

"Yes," said Falconer.

"Do you know the pond at Hampstead Heath?"

"Very well."

"Be there at one o'clock, and bring ten separate packages of ten thousand pounds each. You often pay big sums in cash, your daughter tells me. Get it somehow. Drive yourself, with the money in the boot. If you are followed or have anybody with you, you know what will happen."

"I will be there, alone and not followed," Falconer said frigidly.

Gideon looked across at Hobbs when the telephone rang again, half an hour later, and this time it was Lady Falconer.

"My husband is to meet Robin Kell at the pond on Hampstead Heath," she reported. "He has to have a hundred thousand pounds, in notes, in the boot of his car."

"So you made it," Kell said, his voice almost a sneer.

"I always carry out my obligations," said Falconer, looking beyond the youth to the pond.

"Have you got the money?" Kell demanded.

"Yes."

"How did you get it?"

"I keep a substantial sum in my safe, and as you said, I often pay in cash for purchases. I drew enough from three different banks."

"We're going to Lancelot Judd's shop," said Kell, obviously satisfied. "I've a taxi waiting. And I've friends following and watching. One false move, and that's the end."

"Do you think I value my life so lightly?" demanded Falconer.

"I will say one thing, you've got your priorities right! Your life first, your daughter's second." There was a tone of grudging admiration in Kell's voice. "Get in with me. Somebody will follow in your car."

A taxi drew up alongside, and Falconer had time only to see the youthful face of the driver before getting in. Kell slammed the door and sat back in a corner. After a few moments, he took an envelope from beneath his coat and handed it to Falconer, saying, "See if you recognize those." Falconer drew out some glossy photographs, held them toward the window, and looked down at the top one.

As he looked at them one after another, recognizing them as recently stolen Old Masters, the taxi drove to the shop on the High Street and stopped. Robin put a restraining hand on Falconer's arm, and after a pause an attractive young woman appeared from the shop, smiling serenely.

"All clear," she said.

"In we go," said Kell, "and don't forget what's at stake, Sir Richard!" He half dragged Falconer from the taxi toward the open door, and as they went inside, he muttered: "Upstairs." Another youth was at the foot of the stairs, and at the top was Lancelot Judd, pale faced, gripping the brass rail. Falconer forced himself to walk up the stairs calmly; Kell pushed hard behind him. The shop doorway banged and a key turned in the lock.

On one side was a canvas curtain hanging on a brass pole, and once they were all upstairs, Kell went across and pulled the curtain back very slowly. In front of Falconer's still-unbelieving eyes were eleven canvases, most of them in temporary frames, hanging on the wall of a recess.

Even though Falconer had been prepared for what he was going to see, he still experienced a sense of almost physical shock. There was Vermeer's "Ice Town"; and next to that, Titian's "Head of a Boy." A little further along he recognized Gainsborough's "Lady Lost." Further on again, he saw Botticelli's "Cartoon of the Dying." Each of these had for an age been imprinted on Falconer's mind. Now they, and so many others, seemed to burn into him. He had no doubt at all that they were genuine, and felt as he always did the hypnotic pull of each one, felt his blood turning to water, his knees weakening. He stood very still.

"They're the McCoy all right," said Kell. "Now-the money's in the boot of your car, isn't it? Hand over the key."

"When I have seen my daughter," demurred Falconer.

"*Now*. The only condition was that you saw the other stuff, and you've seen it. Hand it over, or we'll take—"

"You cannot get that boot open without a special key, unless you want an alarm to go off. And I will not give you this key until I have seen Christine, and I am safely back in my own home. This arrangement is not as one-sided as you think, Mr. Kell."

Kell's hand flexed and unflexed, one hovered near his trousers pocket, but suddenly he spun round, strode to another curtain, and pulled it aside.

There was Christine: asleep or drugged. She sat erect in a small chair and she was bound to it. In some way, her head had been tilted backward, emphasizing the flawless line of neck and shoulders, as lovely as her mother's. Nearby, Lance Judd stood rigidly, staring not at the girl but at her father.

"Don't—don't argue anymore," he pleaded. "Don't make it any worse. Give Robin—"

And then there came across his words a wild scream from the girl below.

"The police are coming!" she cried. "The police!"

There was a second of stunned silence before Robin Kell's hand flashed to and from his jacket and the click of his knife sounded loud. Falconer tried to rush forward to protect his daughter, but the knife moved swift as light toward him, and into his belly. He felt a searing pain and staggered to one side, saw the knife flash again as Kell turned to use it on Christine.

But as he did so, the knife moving toward her defenceless throat, Lance Judd hurled himself in front of her, and the knife went into his chest. He gasped, he choked, the door crashed, and the window of the kitchen crashed; then ladders appeared at the upstairs window and police wearing steel helmets smashed the glass. It was Thwaites, running up the stairs, who saw the pictures, saw the trickle of flame run along the way where they were displayed, saw the girl with a taper in her hand stabbing it toward rags that he sensed were soaked in oil. He struck the girl aside and kicked at the blazing rags, and when one fell close to the wall he picked it up with his bare fingers and flung it away.

By then, the place was full of smoke and full of police, and Robin Kell was struggling with two policemen who were trying to prise the knife out of his hand.

Only ten minutes later, a telephone rang on Gideon's desk. Gideon snatched the receiver up eagerly, and as he announced himself, a man said crisply: "It's all over, sir. The girl's all right."

"Falconer?" demanded Gideon, heart thumping with relief.

"A nasty wound in the stomach, sir, and on his way to hospital. So is the man Judd, who tried to save her; he got a knife in his chest. Kell, a girl named Marie Devaux, and others are on their way to the Yard now, sir, for interrogation."

"The pictures?" demanded Gideon sharply.

"Virtually undamaged, sir. I—oh, here's Chief Inspector Thwaites, if you'd like a word with him."

"I would indeed," said Gideon warmly, and a moment later heard Thwaites speak with a feeling that made him seem almost a different man.

"No damage at all really, sir. A frame was scorched, that's all. The young devil meant it all right, but everything we planned went off like clockwork."

Gideon found himself laughing.

"Falconer mightn't feel that," he said.

"If you ask me, sir, he was bloody lucky to get off so lightly, everything considered. I—sorry, sir! I wonder if you will have a word with his wife."

"I'll call her at once," promised Gideon.

He reassured Lady Falconer about her daughter and as much as he could about her husband; then he rang off, sat back and reflected, and sent for Hobbs, who came in with his usual promptitude, and with a bundle of reports. There was so much going through, and already the sense of importance about the Velazquez theft was fading, for it was now actually part of the past. There would be the trial to prepare but that wasn't his job, Gideon reflected. Thank God here *was* a case where they could be absolutely certain that they had the right man!

The Entwhistle file was one of those Hobbs had brought in, and Gideon said: "I thought Honiwell wanted this put aside for a while."

"I brought it in because I've had a word with the Governor at Dartmoor," Hobbs said. "Apparently, Entwhistle is in a bad way. He tried to kill himself in his cell last night. Is there anything we can possibly do to help him?"

"We can't breathe a word until we know for certain," Gideon said gloomily. "I only wish we could. Unless we've evidence enough to bring Eric Greenwood back from a buying trip to India and Pakistan. He's just started from London Airport." When Hobbs shook his head, Gideon put a hand on the file and said: "Leave it with me, I might think of something. Anything else that's urgent?"

"I don't think so," Hobbs answered. "Not to say urgent. There's more than enough to clear up and more than enough pending. I—"

He broke off, for the door opened abruptly, a rare thing in Gideon's office, and Chamberlain came in, with rather less than his usual bounce. He was taken aback at seeing them both together, hesitated, let the door close behind him, and advanced.

"Oh, Commander, in view of the recovery of the Velazquez and the other stolen items, I think we might be well-advised to cancel tomorrow's conference, don't you?"

Gideon, solid as a Buddha in his chair, said: "I think that's a very good idea, sir."

"Good. I thought you would agree. Will you telephone all concerned?"

"If you don't mind my saying so, sir," said Gideon, "I think it would be very much appreciated if you telephoned yourself. I really do."

"Yes, very well," said Chamberlain after a pause. "There are a number of other issues I would like to discuss with you, but perhaps tomorrow would be a better day."

"Whenever you wish," said Gideon.

Neither he nor Hobbs made any comment about the intrusion when Chamberlain left, and Hobbs took out a slim file.

"Lemaitre and Singleton have fixed that raid on the counterfeiters for tonight," he announced. "I've asked them both to send reports to us, so we'll get both sides of the story."

There wasn't much that Hobbs missed, Gideon reflected appreciatively.

When he had gone, Gideon sat back in his chair and pondered. Chamberlain, of course, could not last very long; it was obvious that he was a misfit, and if he didn't realize it himself, Scott-Marie would find a way to make him. Thwaites was a different kind of problem. He was old for promotion but he had done such a dedicated job that it ought to be recognized, and a Superintendent's pension would be considerably higher than a Chief Inspector's. He would put through a recommendation today. He made a note and saw other notes he had made this morning about the conference on the immigration problems. That would need very careful handling.

He saw Thwaites in the middle of the afternoon, his hand heavily bandaged, his hair singed, but an expression of deep contentment in his eyes.

"Congratulations," Gideon said. "Sit down."

"It was all your idea, sir," Thwaites said warmly. "While I was having my hand dressed, I was thinking it must be hell for you - with respect sir - having to sit here knowing you could be out on the job and doing it twice as well as most." He gave Gideon time for only a deprecatory wave and plunged on. "Latest reports, sir: Sir Richard not in danger, I'm glad to say. Knife wound identical with those in Slater and de Courvier, and caused by the same knife, so we've got Kell for murder . . . Lancelot Judd touch and go, sir, but if he pulls through he'll turn queen's evidence without a doubt . . . Christine's suffering from shock, nothing a few days' rest won't put right . . . Not a single item damaged, sir; we picked up a million pounds' worth of stolen works of art. I hope the newspapers make a fuss about that little lot! . . . Oh, and by the way, Falconer's man Oliphant seems to me in a highly nervous condition. I think I'm going to see what he's been up to. A runner I know, Red Thomas, told Division that Oliphant spends a lot of time with Mrs. Bessell in Bond Street. That's about the lot, sir. Oh! There is *one* other offbeat little thing."

"What's that?" asked Gideon.

"Remember Lucy Jenkins, Leslie J.'s daughter? Works for Old Fisky in a shop in the King's road?"

"I pass it every day," Gideon said.

"Well, apparently Lucy bought a load of junk when the old man was away and one of the pictures was a find. Fisky took it round to Division. A John Bettes, stolen from Rosebury House in Suffolk about ten years ago, worth forty or fifty thousand. The insurance company's going to pay out ten per cent reward and Old Fisky's sharing it with Lucy."

"I couldn't be more glad," Gideon said. "I really couldn't."

As he drove home that night, he slowed down alongside Old Fisky's shop, where there were lights, more cars, television cameramen, and Lucy holding up a picture while Old Fisky peered from inside the shop.

She's not a bad-looking girl, Gideon reflected. This could be the making of her.

He noticed a policeman in uniform on the other side of the road, so intent on the scene in the doorway and on Lucy Jenkins that he did not see that the Commander was drawing away. None of the newspaper, television, or press men noticed Gideon, either, but when he reached Harrington Street, half a dozen neighbours waved newspapers at him and Penelope came running out of the house, very excited.

"Daddy, Mummy's told me you're going to soundproof the attic. That's just wonderful. I'd been hoping for something like that. And there's just room to get the piano in. Alec stopped by to see you and heard about it, and he's checked it all for me." She flung her arms round him and kissed him.

And Kate, standing in the doorway to welcome him, could tell that for her husband it had been a deeply satisfying day.

JOHN CREASEY

GIDEON'S DAY

Gideon's day is a busy one. He balances family commitments with solving a series of seemingly unrelated crimes from which a plot nonetheless evolves and a mystery is solved.

One of the most senior officers within Scotland Yard, George Gideon's crime solving abilities are in the finest traditions of London's world famous police headquarters. His analytical brain and sense of fairness is respected by colleagues and villains alike.

'The finest of all Scotland Yard series' – *New York Times*.

GIDEON'S FIRE

Commander George Gideon of Scotland Yard has to deal successively with news of a mass murderer, a depraved maniac, and the deaths of a family in an arson attack on an old building south of the river. This leaves little time for the crisis developing at home ....

'Gideon of Scotland Yard emerges as one of the most real working detectives in modern fiction.... A sympathetic and believable professional policeman.' - *New York Times*

JOHN CREASEY

THE CREEPERS

"The prisoner's hand was thin and bony ... And in the centre of the palm was a pinkish mark. It was the shape of a wolf's head, mouth open, fangs showing. Although it was what he had expected to see, Inspector West felt a twinge of repugnance a stab not unrelated to fear. It was the fifth time he had seen the mark of the wolf – the mark of Lobo."

A gang of cat burglars led by Lobo cause mayhem as they terrorize the city. They must be stopped, but with little in the way of evidence the police are baffled. Just how can Inspector West manage to do this in what is a race against time before more victims succumb?

"Here is an excellent novel of law enforcement officers, harried, discouraged and desperately fatigued, moving inexorably ahead under the pressure of knowledge that they must succeed to save human lives." - Cleveland Plain-Dealer

"Furiously exciting" - Chicago Tribune

"The action is fast, continuous and exciting" - San Francisco News

John Creasey

The House of the Bears

Standing alone in the bleak Yorkshire Moors is Sir Rufus Marne's 'House of the Bears'. Dr. Palfrey is asked to journey there to examine an invalid - who has now disappeared. Moreover, Marne's daughter lies terribly injured after a fall from the minstrel's gallery which Dr. Palfrey discovers was no accident. He sets out to investigate and the results surprise even him . . . .

> *"'Palfrey' and his boys deserve to take their places among the immortals." - Western Mail*

Introducing the Toff

Whilst returning home from a cricket match at his father's country home, the Honourable Richard Rollison - alias The Toff - comes across an accident which proves to be a mystery. As he delves deeper into the matter with his usual perseverance and thoroughness, murder and suspense form the backdrop to a fast moving and exciting adventure.

> *'The Toff has been promoted to a place of honour among amateur detectives.' – The Times Literary Supplement*

Printed in Great Britain
by Amazon